The Life of Lazarillo of Tormes

HIS FORTUNES AND MISFORTUNES

Lazarillo of Tormes

HIS FORTUNES AND MISFORTUNES
❋ *As told by himself*

*Translated, and with an introduction,
by Robert S. Rudder*

With a Sequel by Juan de Luna

*Translated by Robert S. Rudder
with Carmen Criado de Rodríguez Puértolas*

FREDERICK UNGAR PUBLISHING CO.
NEW YORK

ISBN-13: 978-0615961392 (SVENSON Publishers)
ISBN-10: 0615961398

This translation is for

LISA, PAULA,

and

CHRISTOPHER MICHAEL

three small pícaros

Contents

Introduction

Lazarillo of Tormes appeared in sixteenth-century Spain like a breath of fresh air among hundreds of insipidly sentimental novels of chivalry. With so many works full of knights who were manly and brave enough to fight any adversary, but prone to become weak in the knees when they saw their fair lady nearby, was it any wonder that Lazarillo, whose only goal was to fill a realistically hungry stomach, should go straight to the hearts of all Spain. The little novel sold enough copies for three different editions to be issued in 1554, and then was quickly translated into several languages. It initiated a new genre of writing called the "picaresque."

It seems certain that other editions, or at least other manuscripts, of *Lazarillo* were circulating previously, but the earliest we know of were the three published in 1554. One of these was printed at Burgos, another at Antwerp, and the third at Alcala de Henares. They all differ somewhat in language, but it is the one from Alcala de Henares that departs most radically from the other two. It adds some episodes, not in the other editions, which were probably written by a second author.

Because *Lazarillo* was so critical of the clergy, it was put on the Index Purgatorius in 1559 and further editions were prohibited inside Spain. Then, in 1573, an abridged version was printed that omitted Chapters four and five, along with other items displeasing to a watchful Inquisition; later additional episodes were suppressed. This mutilated version was reprinted until the nineteenth century, when Spain finally allowed its people to read the complete work once again.

The identity of the author of this novel has always been a mystery. A few names have been suggested over the years: Juan de Ortega, a Jeronymite monk; Sebastian de Horozco, a dramatist and collector of proverbs. But probably the most widely accepted theory was the attribution to Diego Hurtado de Mendoza, a famous humanist. Many early editions of *Lazarillo* carried his name as author, even though there has never been any real proof of his authorship. Some critics, following Américo Castro's lead, think the author was a Jewish convert to Christianity because of certain phrases which point in that direction. And some think he was a follower of Erasmus, despite the French critic Marcel Bataillon's emphatic statements to the contrary.

One of the first relationships we become aware of as we read this novel is the link of the name Lazaro (Lazarillo: little Lazaro) with the biblical Lazarus: either the figure who died and was brought back to life (John 16) or the beggar (Luke 16:20-31).

This "historical" relationship is further compounded by the fact that many episodes of the novel are versions of material traditional in European folklore. There is, for instance, a thirteenth century French theatrical farce, *Le garcon et l'aveugle*, in which a servant plays tricks on a blind man. And the British Museum manuscript of the *Decretals* of Gregory IX contains an illustration of a boy drinking through a straw from a blind man's bowl. The episode in which Lazarillo thinks a corpse is being brought to his house appears in the *Liber facetiarum et similitudinum Ludovici de Pinedo, et amicorum* and may be a folktale. And the story of the constable and the pardoner is to be found in the fourth novel of *Il novellino* by Masuccio Salernitano, and may also be a folktale.

It has long been said that this novel is an accurate reflection of society in sixteenth-century Spain. And to some extent, this does seem to be true. The king of Spain, Charles I, became involved in several foreign wars, and had gone deeply into debt to German and Italian bankers in order to finance those wars. Soon the quantities of gold and silver coming from Spain's mines in the New World were being sent directly to the foreign bankers. The effects of inflation were to be seen everywhere, as were other social ills. Beggars and beggars' guilds were numerous. Men of all classes were affixing titles to their names, and refusing any work--especially any sort of manual labor--unless it suited their new "rank." The clergy was sadly in need of reform. And pardoners were--often unscrupulously--selling indulgences that granted the forgiveness of sins in return for money to fight the infidel in North Africa and the Mediterranean. All these things are to be found in *Lazarillo of Tormes*.

But is the book really an accurate reflection of all of Spanish society? If there were avaricious priests, and priests who had mistresses, were there none with strong moral principles? If poverty was felt so keenly by Lazarillo and others, was there no one who enjoyed a good meal? As another writer has suggested, the Spanish conquerors did not come to the New World on empty stomachs, nor was the Spanish Armada ill supplied. It is obvious, then, that while *Lazarillo* reflects Spanish society, it mirrors only one segment of that society. Its writer ignored uncorrupted men of generosity and high moral principles who surely existed alongside the others. So just as the chivalresque novels distorted reality upward, this novel distorts reality downward and almost invariably gives us only the negative traits of society.

An important point is the unity, or nonunity, of the book. Earliest critics of Lazarillo of Tormes saw it as a loosely formed novel of unconnected episodes whose only point of unity happened to be the little rogue who told his life story, in which he is seen as serving one master after another. Later criticism has changed that point of view, however, by pointing to such unifying factors as wine, which is used as a recurring theme throughout (Lazarillo steals it; it is used for washing his wounds; he sells it). Then there is the "initiation" in which Lazarillo's head is slammed against a stone statue of a bull. Later the blind man smashes his own head against a stone post as poetic justice is meted out. Finally, Lazarillo's mother will "lie at the side--or stay on the side of good people," and as the novel ends Lazaro decides to do the same.

Claudio Guillén, a modern critic, has noted that time is also a unifying factor in this novel. Early incidents are told in detail, and at moments of pain specific amounts of time are measured ("I felt the pain from its horns for three days"). When Lazarillo is taken in by the squire his hunger pangs become so great that he begins to count the hours. But as conditions improve for Lazarillo's stomach, he gradually forgets about the slow passage of time. In fact, time now begins to race past: four months with the pardoner, four years with the chaplain. This slow, then swift, passage of time is used by Guillén to explain the extreme brevity of some later chapters of the novel. It is a mature Lazaro, he says, who is telling the story and reflecting on his childhood. And we are really seeing the memory process of this older Lazaro who glosses over less important parts of his life and dwells on the moments that matter.

Other critics have responded to the question of "finality" in the work; that is, is Lazarillo an incomplete novel or not? Francisco Rico believes the novel is complete, and that there is a "circular" structure to it all. He notes that the novel is addressed to a certain fictional character ("You": Vuestra merced), and that Lazarillo intends to tell this character "all the details of the matter," the "matter" apparently being the questionable relations between the archpriest and Lazarillo's wife. So there is a continuity from the beginning of the work through the details of Lazarillo's life, until the last chapter ("right up to now") where the "matter" itself, alluded to previously in the Prologue, is finally given in some detail.

Another critic, Américo Castro, points out that *Lazarillo of Tormes* is different from other types of sixteenth century prose fiction in at least one extremely important way that points toward the modern novel. The knights of chivalresque novels and the shepherds who sighed and lamented their way through pastoral novels were flat characters with no room to grow. Not so Lazarillo. Every action, every twist of fortune makes an impression on him, forms his way of looking at the world and shapes his nature. From an innocent little boy he becomes a mischievous, then vengeful, blind man's boy. He observes the hypocrisy, avarice, false pride, materialism of his masters, and when he marries the archpriest's mistress for what he can gain, he applies all the lessons he has learned on the ladder to success-- to the "height of all good fortune." Américo Castro also notes that *Lazarillo of Tormes* is a step toward the masterpiece of Cervantes, *Don Quixote of La Mancha*. As this critic said: "In addition to its intrinsic merits, the *Lazarillo de Tormes* is supremely important viewed in its historic perspective. In many ways it made possible the *Quijote*. Among other things, it offered in the intimate opposition of the squire and his servant the first outline of the duality-unity of Don Quijote and Sancho."

Style is another point of great importance to this novel, particularly in the use of conceits. Lazarillo's father, for example, "suffered persecution for righteousness' sake," a clear reference to the beatitudes. But in this case "righteousness" is the law who is punishing him for being the thief that he is. Throughout the novel we see similar plays on words: the master, who "although he was *blind, enlightened* me;" or the squire who tried to coax certain young ladies one morning, and whose stomach was *warm*, but when he discovered that his pocketbook was *cold*, he suffered *hot-chills*.

It is not surprising that sequels promptly appeared, but the writers of these unfortunately lacked the genius of the author of the original *Lazarillo*. An anonymous sequel appeared in 1555 with the title, *The Second Part of Lazarillo of Tormes, His Fortunes and Misfortunes*. Its beginning words are the same as the final ones of the first *Lazarillo*, but there any similarity ends. In this novel Lazaro makes friends with some Germans and his wife gives birth to a daughter. Lazaro then enlists to go on an expedition to fight the Turks, his ship sinks, and he is miraculously changed into a fish. He has many adventures in the sea, and is finally caught up in the nets of some fishermen and changes back into a man. The novel is a fantasy, and may be allegorical. The beginning is its most realistic point, and the first chapter of this novel became tacked onto the end of the first *Lazarillo*.

No further sequels were printed until 1620 when Juan Cortes de Tolosa's book, *Lazarillo de Manzanares*, was published. This novel imitates the first *Lazarillo* in its initial episodes, but is again far less successful than the original.

In the same year, 1620, Juan de Luna's *Second Part of the Life of Lazarillo of Tormes* was published in Paris. (Another edition was published simultaneously in Paris, but was marked as though printed in Zaragoza to facilitate the book's sale in Spain.) Little is definitely known about Luna. We do know that he was born in Spain (Toledo). He apparently fled to France in 1612 as a political and religious refugee: in one of his books he refers to himself as "a foreigner who has left behind his homeland, his relatives, and his estate for a just and legitimate cause." It has been speculated that Luna may have been educated for the priesthood but then grown dissatisfied and even vehemently bitter toward the clergy. The reason for his flight to France has been interpreted as a flight from the Spanish Inquisition. In France, in Montauban, he began to study theology to prepare himself for the Protestant ministry. But soon afterward he became a Spanish teacher in Paris, and in 1619 published a book of proverbs and phrases for Spanish students. The following year his continuation of Lazarillo was published, along with a revised version of the original Lazarillo (revised because its style did not suit his tastes). Next he appeared in London, in 1622, attempting to have his sequel translated into English. His Spanish grammar was published there the following year. The last information we have of him is that he became a Protestant minister in England, and for three years delivered sermons to his fellow Spaniards each Sunday, in Mercer's Chapel, Cheapside, London.

Although the details of Juan de Luna's life are rather sketchy, a great deal more can be said about his novel. His continuation of Lazarillo was the only sequel to meet with any success. The same characters--Lazarillo, the archpriest, the squire, etc.--are here, but their personalities are changed drastically. The squire is the one who is most noticeably different. He is no longer the sympathetic, poor, generous (when he has money) figure of the first part. Now he is a thief, a cowardly braggart, a dandy, and Lazaro has nothing but scorn for him. Lazaro himself is now fully grown, and there is no room for his personality to change as before. Perhaps the only character who is still the same is Lazaro's wife.

Other differences between the two novels are also evident. In the first *Lazarillo* we see a central protagonist who serves a different master or performs a different type of work in each chapter. But in Luna's sequel we do not have this same structure. In the first five chapters of Luna's book, for example, Lazarillo's adventures flow as they do in traditional novels: he goes to sea, the ship sinks, he is captured by fishermen and put on exhibition as a fish, and finally he is rescued. The following chapters, however, often divide his life into segments as he goes from one position to another.

Another difference to be noted is that while the first Lazarillo addresses a certain person ("You": Vuestra merced) who is not the reader but an acquaintance of the archpriest, in the *Second Part* something quite different occurs. Luna's Lazaro addresses the "dear reader" but hardly with flattering terms: he humorously suggests that we may all be cuckolds. Then he ironically refuses to tell us about--or even let us think about--certain promiscuous details because they may offend our pure and pious ears. The framework of the first novel is apparently a device whose purpose, like the "Arabic historian" and the "translators" of *Don Quixote*, is to create an atmosphere of realism, while Luna's "dear reader" is simply a device for humor.

Another important distinction to be made between the two books is the extent of word-play used. Almost one hundred years elapsed between the times the two books were published, and literary styles changed a great deal. While the first *Lazarillo* used some conceits, as we have previously noted, Luna's book abounds with them to the point where it becomes baroque. About people who are being flooded with water or are drowning, it is usually said that they are overcome by trifling, but watery, circumstances: "a drop in the ocean" (ahogar en tan poca agua). Lazarillo's child is "born with the odor of saintliness about her" (una hija ingerta a cañutillo); unfortunately this refers less to her as holy than it does to the fact that her father is really the archpriest. The use of antithesis is also evident throughout Luna's novel. From the beginning in which he dedicated his small work to a great princess, throughout the length of the book, we find Lazaro esteemed by his friends and feared by his enemies, begging from people who give money with open hands while he does not take it with closed ones, and so on. Another trick in language is Luna's plays on sounds: such combinations as salí--salté (left--leaped), comedia--comida (rituals--victuals) are abundant. Luna also uses obscene conceits for a humorous purpose, mixing them with religious allusions both for humor and to vent his own feelings of hostility against the church.

Yet another important difference between the two novels lies in Luna's emphasis on tying up loose ends. We know that in the first *Lazarillo* the protagonist leaves the blind man for dead, not knowing what happened to him, and we never do find out whether he survived the blow or not. Later the squire runs away from Lazaro, and we never see him again either. The author of the first *Lazarillo* gives us a series of vignettes in which the psychological interplay of the characters is stressed. The characters fade out of Lazaro's life just as people fade in and out of our own lives. Luna, however, was much more interested in telling a good story--and one that has an ending. So the squire appears, and tells what happened to him after leaving Lazaro: a complete story in itself. He steals Lazaro's clothes and runs off, and later we see him again--having got his just retribution almost by pure chance. The inn-keeper's daughter runs off with her priest, and both turn up several chapters later; their account amounts to another short story. The "innocent" girl and the bawd disappear, then return to play a scene with Lazaro once more, and finally they fade out, presumably to live by their wits ever after. Related to this stress on external action is the importance Luna gives to descriptive rather than psychological detail. His minutely detailed descriptions of clothing are especially noteworthy: the squire's "suit"; the gallant's clothing as he emerges from the trunk; the costume worn by the girl who became a gypsy. These are descriptions we do not find in the original *Lazarillo* because the author of that work is much more interested in internal motivations than external description and action.

Let us move on to another point: the social satire in the two novels. We have seen the satire against the various classes, and particularly against the church, in the first *Lazarillo*. And Luna's satire has the same targets. The essential difference is in the way the two authors handle their darts. The first *Lazarillo* is fairly subtle in its attacks: men are avaricious, materialistic unscrupulous infamous--and these vices are sometimes only very loosely connected with the church. But Luna wants us to know definitely that the church is like this, so his satire of the church is blunt and devastating. The Inquisition, he tells us plainly, is corrupt, brutal, and feared throughout all of Spain. Priests and friars are always anxious to accept a free meal, they have mistresses, and they are less principled than thieves. Lawyers and the entire judicial system are corrupt. The Spaniards, Luna tells us from his position of exile in Paris, are too proud to work, and they will become beggars rather than perform any sort of manual labor. Lazaro himself is held up to us as a "mirror of Spanish sobriety." Apparently Luna's anger about having to leave Spain had no opportunity to mellow before he finished his novel.

Luna's *Second Part of Lazarillo of Tormes* is not the "First Part." But even so, it has its merit.

Luna liked to tell stories, and he was good at it. Some scenes are witty and highly entertaining. When Lazaro meets his old friends, the bawd and the "maiden," at an inn, the action is hardly dull. The "quarter of kid" becomes the center of attraction from the time it appears on Lazaro's plate until he falls and ejects it from his throat, and it is used skillfully and humorously to tell us a great deal about each of the characters present.

Another scene worth calling to the reader's special attention is the chapter in which a feast is held that erupts into a brawl, after which the local constabulary arrives. Luna's account is a very close predecessor of the modern farce. Many of the elements seem to be present: a lack of reverence, a situation used for comic effects, the chase through many rooms to find the guests, the beatings that the constable's men are given by the pursued, being "breaded" in flour, "fried" in oil, and left out on the street where they run away, ashamed to be seen. It is as though we are catching a glimpse of the Keystone Cops, seventeenth-century style. And the variations from seventeenth to twentieth century do not appear to amount to a great deal.

-ROBERT S. RUDDER

University of California at Los Angeles
December 1972

Translator's Note

My translation of the first *Lazarillo* follows Foulché Delbosc's edition, which attempts to restore the *editio princeps* but does not include the interpolations of the Alcalá de Henares edition. The translation of the first chapter of the anonymous sequel of 1555 follows at the end of the first part because it serves as a bridge between the first novel and Luna's sequel. For Juan de Luna's sequel, the modern edition by Elmer Richard Sims, more faithful to the manuscript than any other edition, has been utilized.

A word of thanks is due to Professor Julio Rodríguez Puértolas, whose own work was so often interrupted by questions from the outer sanctum, and who nevertheless bore through it all with good humor, and was very helpful in clearing up certain mysteries in the text.

The seventy-three drawings were prepared by Leonard Bramer, a Dutch painter who was born in 1596 and died in 1674. Living most of his life in Delft, he is best known for his drawings and for his illustrations of Ovid's writings and of other works of literature. The original drawings are in the keeping of the Graphische Sammlung in Munich, and are used here by permission.

R.S.R.

The Life of Lazarillo of Tormes,
His Fortunes
and Misfortunes

θ

As told by himself

Prologue

I think it is good that such remarkable things as these, which may never have been heard of or seen before, should come to the attention of many people instead of being buried away in the tomb of oblivion. Because it might turn out that someone who reads about them will like what he reads, and even people who only glance lightly through this book may be entertained.

Pliny says along these lines that there is no book--no matter how bad it is--that doesn't have something good in it. And this is all the more true since all tastes are not the same: what one man won't even touch, another will be dying to get. And so there are things that some people don't care for, while others do. The point is that nothing should be destroyed or thrown away unless it is really detestable; instead, it should be shown to everybody, especially if it won't do any harm and they might get some good out of it.

If this weren't so, there would be very few people who would write for only one reader, because writing is hardly a simple thing to do. But since writers go ahead with it, they want to be rewarded, not with money but with people seeing and reading their works, and if there is something worthwhile in them, they would like some praise. Along these lines too, Cicero says: "Honor promotes the arts."

Does anyone think that the first soldier to stand up and charge the enemy hates life? Of course not; a craving for glory is what makes him expose himself to danger. And the same is true in arts and letters. The young preacher gives a very good sermon and is really interested in the improvement of people's souls, but ask his grace if he minds when they tell him, "Oh, what an excellent sermon you gave today, Reverend!" And So-and-so was terrible in jousting today, but when some rascal praised him for the way he had handled his weapons, he gave him his armor. What would he have done if it had really been true?

And so everything goes: I confess that I'm no more saintly than my neighbors, but I would not mind it at all if those people who find some pleasure in this little trifle of mine (written in my crude style) would get wrapped up in it and be entertained by it, and if they could see that a man who has had so much bad luck and so many misfortunes and troubles does exist.

Please take this poor effort from a person who would have liked to make it richer if only his ability had been as great as his desire. And since you told me that you wanted me to write down all the details of the matter, I have decided not to start out in the middle but at the beginning. That way you will have a complete picture of me, and at the same time those people who received a large inheritance will see how little they had to do with it, since fortune favored them, and they will also see how much more those people accomplished whose luck was going against them, since they rowed hard and well and brought their ship safely into port.

I - Lazaro Tells about His Life and His Parents

You should know first of all that I'm called Lazaro of Tormes, and that I'm the son of Tome Gonzales and Antona Perez, who were born in Tejares, a village near Salamanca. I was actually born in the Tormes River, and that's how I got my name. It happened this way: My father (God rest his soul) was in charge of a mill on the bank of that river, and he was the miller there for more than fifteen years. Well, one night while my mother was in the mill, carrying me around in her belly, she went into labor and gave birth to me right there. So I can really say I was born in the river.

Then when I was eight years old, they accused my father of gutting the sacks that people were bringing to the mill. They took him to jail, and without a word of protest he went ahead and confessed everything, and he suffered persecution for righteousness' sake. But I trust God that he's in heaven because the Bible calls that kind of man blessed. At that time they were getting together an expedition to go fight the Moors, and my father went with them. They had exiled him because of the bad luck that I've already told about, so he went along as a muleteer for one of the men, and like a loyal servant, he ended his life with his master.

My widowed mother, finding herself without a husband or anyone to take care of her, decided to lie at the side--I mean, stay on the side--of good men and be like them. So she came to the city to live. She rented a little house and began to cook for some students. She washed clothes for some stableboys who served the Commander of La Magdalena, too, so a lot of the time she was around the stables. She and a dark man--one of those men who took care of the animals-- got to know each other. Sometimes he would come to our house and wouldn't leave till the next morning; and other times he would come to our door in the daytime pretending that he wanted to buy eggs, and then he would come inside.

When he first began to come I didn't like him, he scared me because of the color of his skin and the way he looked. But when I saw that with him around there the food got better, I began to like him quite a lot. He always brought bread and pieces of meat, and in the winter he brought in firewood so we could keep warm.

So with his visits and the relationship going right along, it happened that my mother gave

7

me a pretty little black baby, and I used to bounce it on my knee and help keep it warm.

I remember one time when my black stepfather was playing with the little fellow, the child noticed that my mother and I were white but that my stepfather wasn't and he got scared. He ran to my mother and pointed his finger at him and said, "Mama, it's the bogeyman!" And my stepfather laughed: "You little son-of-a-bitch!"

Even though I was still a young boy, I thought about the word my little brother had used, and I said to myself: How many people there must be in the world who run away from others when they don't see themselves.

As luck would have it, talk about Zaide (that was my stepfather's name) reached the ears of the foreman, and when a search was made they found out that he'd been stealing about half of the barley that was supposed to be given to the animals. He'd pretended that the bran, wood, currycombs, aprons, and the horse covers and blankets had been lost; and when there was nothing else left to steal, he took the shoes right off the horses' hooves. And he was using all this to buy things for my mother so that she could bring up my little brother.

Why should we be surprised at priests when they steal from the poor or at friars when they take things from their monasteries to give to their lady followers, or for other things, when we see how love can make a poor slave do what he did?

And they found him guilty of everything I've said and more because they asked me questions and threatened me too, and I answered them like a child. I was so frightened that I told them everything I knew--even about some horseshoes my mother had made me sell to a blacksmith.

They beat and tarred my poor stepfather, and they gave my mother a stiff sentence besides the usual hundred lashes: they said that she couldn't go into the house of the Commander (the one I mentioned) and that she couldn't take poor Zaide into her own house.

So that matters wouldn't get any worse, the poor woman went ahead and carried out the sentence. And to avoid any danger and get away from wagging tongues, she went to work as a servant for the people who were living at the Solano Inn then. And there, while putting up with all kinds of indignities, she managed to raise my little brother until he knew how to walk. And she even raised me to be a good little boy who would take wine and candles to the guests and do whatever else they told me.

About this time a blind man came by and stayed at the inn. He thought I would be a good guide for him, so he asked my mother if I could serve him, and she said I could. She told him what a good man my father had been and how he'd died in the battle of Gelves for the holy faith. She said she trusted God that I wouldn't turn out any worse a man than my father, and she begged him to be good to me and look after me, since I would be an orphan now. He told her he would and said that I wouldn't be a servant to him, but a son. And so I began to serve and guide my new old master.

After he had been in Salamanca a few days, my master wasn't happy with the amount of money he was taking in, and he decided to go somewhere else. So when we were ready to leave, I went to see my mother. And with both of us crying she gave me her blessing and said, "Son, I know that I'll never see you again. Try to be good, and may God be your guide. I've raised you and given you to a good master; take good care of yourself."

And then I went back out to my master who was waiting for me.

We left Salamanca and we came to a bridge; and at the edge of this bridge there's a stone statue of an animal that looks something like a bull. The blind man told me to go up next to the animal, and when I was there he said, "Lazaro, put your ear up next to this bull and you'll hear a great sound inside of it."

I put my ear next to it very simply, thinking he was telling the truth. And when he felt my head near the statue, he doubled up his fist and knocked my head into that devil of a bull so hard that I felt the pain from its horns for three days. And he said to me, "You fool, now learn that a blind man's servant has to be one step ahead of the devil." And he laughed out loud at his joke.

It seemed to me that at that very instant I woke up from my childlike simplicity and I said to myself, "He's right. I've got to open my eyes and be on my guard. I'm alone now, and I've got to think about taking care of myself."

We started on our way again, and in just a few days he taught me the slang thieves use. When he saw what a quick mind I had he was really happy, and he said, "I can't give you any gold or silver, but I can give you plenty of hints on how to stay alive." And that's exactly what he did; after God, it was this fellow who gave me life and who, although he was blind, enlightened me and showed me how to live.

I like to tell you these silly things to show what virtue there is in men being able to raise themselves up from the depths, and what a vice it is for them to let themselves slip down from high stations.

Well, getting back to my dear blind man and telling about his ways, you should know that from the time God created the world there's no one He made smarter or sharper than that man. At his job he was sly as a fox. He knew over a hundred prayers by heart. He would use a low

tone, calm and very sonorous, that would make the church where he was praying echo. And whenever he prayed, he would put on a humble and pious expression--something he did very well. And he wouldn't make faces or grimaces with his mouth or eyes the way others do.

Besides this he had thousands of other ways of getting money. He told everyone that he knew prayers for lots of different things: for women who couldn't have children or who were in labor; for those women who weren't happy in their marriage--so that their husbands would love them more. He would give predictions to expectant mothers about whether they would have a boy or a girl. And as far as medicine was concerned, he said that Galen never knew the half of what he did about toothaches, fainting spells, and female illnesses. In fact, there was no one who would tell him they were sick that he couldn't immediately say to them: "Do this, and then is; take this herb, or take that root."

And so everyone came to him--especially women--and they believed everything he told them. He got a lot out of them with these ways I've been telling about; in fact, he earned more in a month than a hundred ordinary blind men earn in a year.

But I want you to know, too, that even with all he got and all that he had, I've never seen a more greedy, miserly man. He was starving me to death. He didn't even give me enough to keep me alive! I'm telling the truth: If I hadn't known how to help myself with my wily ways and some pretty clever tricks, I would have died of hunger lots of times. But with all his know-how and carefulness I outwitted him, so that I always--or usually--really got the better of him. The way I did this was I played some devilish tricks on him, and I'll tell about some of them, even though I didn't come out on top every time.

He carried the bread and all the other things in a cloth bag, and he kept the neck of it closed with an iron ring that had a padlock and key. And when he put things in or took them out, he did it so carefully and counted everything so well that no one in the world could have gotten a crumb from him. So I'd take what little he gave me, and in less than two mouthfuls it would be gone.

After he had closed the lock and forgotten about it, thinking that I was busy with other things, I would begin to bleed the miserly bag dry. There was a little seam on the side of the bag that I'd rip open and sew up again. And I would take out bread-- not little crumbs, either, but big hunks--and I'd get bacon and sausage too. And so I was always looking for the right time to score, not on a ball field, but on the food in that blasted bag that the tyrant of a blind man kept away from me.

And then, every time I had a chance I'd steal half copper coins. And when someone gave him a copper to say a prayer for them--and since he couldn't see--they'd no sooner have offered it than I would pop it into my mouth and have a half-copper ready. And as soon as he stuck out his hand, there was my coin reduced to half price. Then the old blind man would start growling at me. As soon as he felt it and realized that it wasn't a whole copper he'd say, "How the devil is it that now that you're with me they never give me anything but half coppers, when they almost always used to give me a copper or a two-copper piece? I'd swear that this is all your fault."

He used to cut his prayers short, too; he wouldn't even get halfway through them. He told me to pull on the end of his cloak whenever the person who asked for the prayer had gone. So that's what I did. Then he'd begin to call out again with his cry, "Who would like to have me say a prayer for him?" in his usual way.

And he always put a little jug of wine next to him when we ate. I would grab it quickly and give it a couple of quiet kisses before I put it back in its place. But that didn't go on for very long: he could tell by the number of nips he took that some was missing. So to keep his wine safe he never let the jug out of reach; he'd always hold on to the handle. But not even a magnet could attract the way I could with a long rye straw that I had made for that very purpose. And I'd stick it in the mouth of the jug and suck until--good-bye, wine! But the old traitor was so wary that I think he must have sensed me, because from then on he stopped that and put the jug between

his legs. And even then he kept his hand over
the top to make sure.

But I got so used to drinking wine that I
was dying for it. And when I saw that my straw
trick wouldn't work, I decided to make a spout
by carving a little hole in the bottom of the jug
and then sealing it off neatly with a little thin
strip of wax. When it was mealtime, I'd pretend
I was cold and get in between the legs of the
miserable blind man to warm up by the little fire
we had. And the heat of it would melt the wax,

since it was such a tiny piece. Then the wine would begin to trickle from the spout into my mouth, and I got into a position so that I wouldn't miss a blasted drop. When the poor fellow went to drink he wouldn't find a thing. He'd draw back, astonished, then he'd curse and damn the jar and the wine, not knowing what could have happened.

"You can't say that I drank it, Sir," I said, "since you never let it out of your hand."

But he kept turning the jug around and feeling it, until he finally discovered the hole and saw through my trick. But he pretended that he hadn't found out.

Then one day I was tippling on my jug as usual, without realizing what was in store for me or even that the blind man had found me out. I was sitting the same as always, taking in those sweet sips, my face turned toward the sky and my eyes slightly closed so I could really savor the delicious liquor. The dirty blind man saw that now was the time to take out his revenge on me, and he raised that sweet and bitter jug with both his hands and smashed it down on my mouth with all his might. As I say, he used all his strength, and poor Lazaro hadn't been expecting anything like this; in fact, I was drowsy and happy as always. So it seemed like the sky and everything in it had really fallen down on top of me. The little tap sent me reeling and knocked me unconscious, and that enormous jug was so huge that pieces of it stuck in my face, cutting me in several places and knocking out my teeth, so that I don't have them to this very day.

From that minute I began to hate that old blind man. Because, even though he took care of me and treated me all right and fixed me up, I saw that he had really enjoyed his dirty trick. He used wine to wash the places where the pieces of the jug had cut me, and he smiled and said, "How about that, Lazaro? The very thing that hurt you is helping to cure you." And he made other witty remarks that I didn't particularly care for.

When I had about recovered from the beating and the black and blue marks were nearly gone, I realized that with a few more blows like that the blind man would have gotten rid of me. So I decided to be rid of him. But I didn't run away right then; I waited until I could do it in a safer and better way. And although I wanted to be kind and forgive the blind man for hitting me with the jug, I couldn't because of the harsh treatment he gave me from then on. Without any reason he would hit me on the head and yank on my hair. And if anyone asked him why he beat me so much, he would tell them about the incident with the jug: "Do you think this boy of mine is just some innocent little fellow? Well, listen and see if you think the devil himself would try anything like this."

After they'd heard about it, they would cross themselves and say, "Well--who would ever think that such a little boy would do anything like that!"

Then they'd laugh at the prank and tell him, "Go on, beat him. God will give you your reward."

And this advice he followed to the letter.

So, for revenge, I'd lead him down all the worst roads on purpose to see if he wouldn't get hurt somehow. If there were rocks, I'd take him right over them; if there was mud, I'd lead him through the deepest part. Because even though I didn't keep dry myself, I would have given an eye if I could have hurt two eyes of that man who didn't even have one. Because of this, he was always beating me with the end of his cane so that my head was full of bumps, and with him always pulling on my hair a lot of it was gone. I told him I wasn't doing it on purpose and that I just couldn't find any better roads, but that didn't do any good. The old traitor saw through everything and was so wary that he wouldn't believe me any more.

So that you can see how smart this shrewd blind man was, I'll tell you about one of the many times when I was with him that he really seemed to show a lot of perception. When we left Salamanca, his plan was to go to Toledo because the people were supposed to be richer there, although not very free with their money. But he pinned his hopes on this saying: "You'll get more water from a narrow flowing stream than you will from a deep dry well." And we'd pass through the best places as we went along. Where we were welcomed and were able to get something, we stayed; where this didn't happen, we'd move on after a few days.

    And it happened that as we were coming to a place called Almorox when they were gathering the grapes, a grape picker gave him a bunch as alms. And since the baskets are usually handled pretty roughly and the grapes were very ripe at the time, the bunch started to fall apart in his hand. If we had thrown it in the sack, it and everything it touched would have spoiled. He decided that we'd have a picnic so that it wouldn't go to waste-- and he did it to please me, too, since he'd kicked and beat me quite a bit that day. So we sat down on a low wall, and he said: "Now I want to be generous with you: we'll share this bunch of grapes, and you can eat as many as I do. We'll divide it like this: you take one, then I'll take one. But you have to promise me that you won't take more than one at a time. I'll do the same until we finish, and that way there won't be any cheating."

The agreement was made, and we began. But on his second turn, the traitor changed his mind and began to take two at a time, evidently thinking that I was doing the same. But when I saw that he had broken our agreement, I wasn't satisfied with going at his rate of speed. Instead, I went even further: I took two at a time, or three at a time--in fact, I ate them as fast as I could. And when there weren't any grapes left, he just sat there for a while with the stem in his hand, and then he shook his head and said, "Lazaro, you tricked me. I'll swear to God that you ate these grapes three at a time."

"No, I didn't," I said. "But why do you think so?"

That wise old blind man answered, "Do you know how I see that you ate them three at a time? Because I was eating them two at a time, and you didn't say a word."

I laughed to myself, and even though I was only a boy, I was very much aware of the sharpness of that blind man.

But, so that I won't talk too much, I won't tell about a lot of humorous and interesting things that happened to me with my first master. I just want to tell about how we separated, and be done with him.

We were in Escalona, a town owned by the duke of that name, at an inn, and the blind man gave me a piece of sausage to roast for him.

When the sausage had been basted and he had sopped up and eaten the drippings with a piece of bread, he took a coin out of his purse and told me to go get him some wine from the tavern. Then the devil put an idea in my head, just like they say he does to thieves. It so happened that near the fire there was a little turnip, kind of long and beat up; it had probably been thrown there because it wasn't good enough for stew. At that moment he and I were there all alone, and when I whiffed the delicious odor of the sausage, I suddenly got a huge appetite-- and I knew that all I would get of it would be the smell.

But the thought of eating that sausage made me lose all my fear: I didn't think for a minute what would happen to me. So while the blind man was getting the money out of his purse, I took the sausage off the spit and quickly put the turnip on. Then the blind man gave me the money for the wine and took hold of the spit, turning it over the fire, trying to cook the very thing that hadn't been cooked before because it was so bad.

I went for the wine, and on the way I downed the sausage. When I came back I found that sinner of a blind man holding the turnip between two slices of bread. He didn't know what it was yet, because he hadn't felt of it. But when he took the bread and bit into it, thinking he would get part of the sausage too, he was suddenly stopped cold by the taste of the cold turnip. He got mad then, and said, "What is this, Lazarillo?"

"You mean, 'Lacerated,'" I said. "Are you trying to pin something on me? Didn't I just come back from getting the wine? Someone must have been here and played a joke on you."

"Oh, no," he said. "I haven't let the spit out of my hand. No one could have done that."

I kept swearing that I hadn't done any switching around. But it didn't do me any good--I couldn't hide anything from the sharpness of that miserable blind man. He got up and grabbed me by the head and got close so he could smell me. And he must have smelled my breath like a good hound. Really being anxious to find out if he was right, he held on tight and opened my mouth wider than he should have. Then, not very wisely, he stuck in his nose. And it was long and sharp. And his anger had made it swell a bit, so that the point of it hit me in the throat. So with all this and my being really frightened, along with the fact that the black sausage hadn't had time to settle in my stomach, and especially with the sudden poking in of his

25

very large nose, half choking me--all these things went together and made the crime and the snack show themselves, and the owner got back what belonged to him. What happened was that before the blind man could take his beak out of my mouth, my stomach got so upset that it hit his nose with what I had stolen. So his nose and the black, half-chewed sausage both left my mouth at the same time.

Oh, Almighty God! I was wishing I'd been buried at that very moment, because I was already dead. The perverse blind man was so mad that if people hadn't come at the noise, I think he would have killed me. They pulled me out of his hands, and he was left with what few hairs had still been in my head. My face was all scratched up, and my neck and throat were clawed. But my throat really deserved its rough treatment because it was only on account of what it had done that I'd been beaten. Then that rotten blind man told everyone there about the things I'd done, and he told them over and over about the jug and the grapes and this last incident.

They laughed so hard that all the people who were going by in the street came in to see the fun. But the blind man told them about my tricks with such wit and cleverness that, even though I was hurt and crying, I felt that it would have been wrong for me not to laugh too.

And while this was going on I suddenly remembered that I'd been negligent and cowardly, and I began to swear at myself: I should have bitten off his nose. I'd had the opportunity to do it; in fact, half of the work had already been done for me. If only I'd clamped down with my teeth, I'd have had it trapped. Even though it belonged to that skunk, my stomach would probably have held it better than it held the sausage; and since there wouldn't have been any evidence, I could have denied the crime. I wish to God I'd have done it. It wouldn't have been a bad idea at all!

The lady running the inn and the others there made us stop our fighting, and they washed my face and throat with the wine I'd brought for him to drink. Then the dirty blind man made up jokes about it, saying things like: "The truth of the matter is I use more wine washing this boy in one year than I drink in two." And: "At least, Lazaro, you owe more to wine than you do to your father-- he only gave you life once, but wine has brought you to life a thousand times."

Then he told about all the times he'd beaten me and scratched my face and then doctored me up with wine.

And the people who were washing me laughed out loud, while I was swearing.

But the blind man's prophecy wasn't wrong, and since then I've often thought about that man who must have had a gift for telling the future. And I feel sorry about the bad things I did to him, although I really paid him back, since what he told me that day happened just like he said it would, as you'll see later on.

Because of this and the dirty tricks the blind man played on me, I decided to leave him for good. And since I had thought about it and really had my mind set on it, this last trick of his only made me more determined. So the next day we went into town to beg. It had rained quite a bit the night before, and since it was still raining that day, he went around praying under the arcades in the town so we wouldn't get wet. But with night coming on and there still being no let up, the blind man said to me, "Lazaro, this rain isn't going to stop, and the later it gets the harder it's coming down. Let's go inside the inn before there's a real downpour."

To get there we had to cross over a ditch that was full of water from the rain. And I said to him; "Sir, the water's too wide to cross here, but if you'd like, I see an easier place to get across, and we won't get wet either. It's very narrow there, and if we jump we'll keep our feet dry."

That seemed like a good idea to him, and he said, "You're pretty clever. That's why I like you so much. Take me to the place where the ditch is narrow. It's winter now, and I don't care for water any time, and especially not when I get my feet wet."

Seeing that the time was ripe, I led him under the arcades, to a spot right in front of a sort of pillar or stone post that was in the plaza-- one of those that hold up the overhanging arches of the houses. And I said to him, "Sir, this is the narrowest place along the whole ditch."

It was really raining hard and the poor man was getting wet. This, along with the fact that we were in a hurry to get out of the water that was pouring down on us--and especially because God clouded his mind so I could get revenge--made him believe me, and he said, "Point me in the right direction, and you jump over the water."

I put him right in front of the pillar. Then I jumped and got behind the post like someone waiting for a bull to charge, and I said to him, "Come on, jump as far as you can so you'll miss the water."

As soon as I'd said that, the poor blind man charged like an old goat. First he took one step back to get a running start, and then he hurled himself forward with all his might. His head hit the post with a hollow sound like a pumpkin. Then he fell over backward, half dead, with his head split open.

"What? You mean to say you smelled the sausage but not the post? Smell it, smell it!" I said, and I left him in the hands of all the people who had run to help him.

I reached the village gate on the run, and before night fell I made it to Torrijos. I didn't know what God had done with him, and I never made any attempt to find out.

II - How Lazaro Took up with a Priest and the Things That Happened to Him with That Man

I didn't feel very safe in that town, so the next day I went to a place named Maqueda. There I met up with a priest (it must have been because of all my sins). I started to beg from him, and he asked me if I knew how to assist at mass. I told him I did, and it was the truth: even though that sinner of a blind man beat me, he'd taught me all kinds of good things, too, and this was one of them. So the priest took me in, and I was out of the frying pan and into the fire. Because even though the blind man was the very picture of greed, as I've said, he was an Alexander the Great compared to this fellow. I won't say any more, except that all the miserliness in the world was in this man. I don't know if he'd been born that way, or if it came along with his priest's frock.

He had an old chest that he kept locked, and he kept the key tied to his cassock with a leather cord. When the holy bread was brought from church, he'd throw it in the chest and lock it up again. And there wasn't a thing to eat in the whole place, the way there is in most houses: a bit of bacon hanging from the chimney, some cheese lying on the table or in the cupboard, a basket with some slices of bread left over from dinner. It seemed to me that even if I hadn't eaten any of it, I would have felt a lot better just being able to look at it.

The only thing around was a string of onions, and that was kept locked in a room upstairs. I was rationed out one onion every four days. And if anyone else was around when I asked him for the key to get it, he'd reach into his breast pocket and untie the key with great airs, and he'd hand it to me and say, "Here. Take it, but bring it back as soon as you're through, and don't stuff yourself." And this as if all the oranges in Valencia were up there, while there really wasn't a damned thing, as I said, besides the onions hanging from a nail. And he had those counted so well that if I (being the sinner that I am) had taken even one extra onion, I would really have been in for it.

So there I was, dying of hunger. But if he wasn't very charitable to me, he was to himself. A good five coppers' worth of meat was his usual fare for supper. I have to admit that he did give me some of the soup, but as for the meat--I didn't even get a whiff of it. All I got was a little bread: that blasted man wouldn't give me half of what I really needed! And on Saturdays everyone around here eats head of mutton, and he sent me for one that cost six coppers. He cooked it and ate the eyes, the tongue, the neck, the brains and the meat in the jaws. Then he gave me the chewed-over bones; he put them on a plate and said, "Here, eat this and be happy. It's a meal fit for a king. In fact, you're living better than the Pope."

"May God grant you this kind of life," I said under my breath.

After I had been with him for three weeks, I got so skinny that my legs wouldn't hold me up out of sheer hunger. I saw that I was heading right straight for the grave if God and my wits didn't come to my rescue. But there was no way I could trick him because there wasn't a thing I could steal. And even if there had been something, I couldn't blind him the way I did the other one (may he rest in peace if that blow on the head finished him off). Because even though the other fellow was smart, without that valuable fifth sense he couldn't tell what I was doing. But this new guy--there isn't anyone whose sight was as good as his was.

When we were passing around the offering plate, not a penny fell into the basket that he didn't have it spotted. He kept one eye on the people and the other on my hands. His eyes danced in their sockets like quicksilver. Every cent that was put in was ticked off in his mind. And as soon as the offering was over, he would take the plate away from me and put it on the altar.

I wasn't able to get a penny away from him all the time I lived with him--or, to be more precise, all the time I died with him. He never sent me to the tavern for even a drop of wine: what little he brought back from the offering and put in the chest he rationed out so that it lasted him a whole week. And to cover up his terrible stinginess, he would say to me, "Look, son, we priests have to be very moderate in our eating and drinking, and that's why I don't indulge the way other people do." But that old miser was really lying, because when we prayed at meetings or at funerals and other people were paying for the food, he ate like a wolf and drank more than any old, thirsty quack doctor.

Speaking of funerals, God forgive me but I was never an enemy of mankind except during them. This was because we really ate well and I was able to gorge myself. I used to hope and pray that God would kill off someone every day. We'd give the sacraments to the sick people, and the priest would ask everyone there to pray. And I was certainly not the last to begin--especially at extreme unction. With all my heart and soul I prayed to God--not that His will be done, as they say, but that He take the person from this world.

And when one of them escaped (God forgive me), I damned him to hell a thousand times. But when one died, I blessed him just as much. Because in all the time that I was there--which must have been nearly six months--only twenty people died. And I really think that I killed them; I mean, they died at my request. Because I think that the Lord must have seen my own endless and awful dying, and He was glad to kill them so that I could live. But at that time I couldn't find any relief for my misery. If I came to life on the days that we buried someone, I really felt the pangs of hunger when there wasn't

any funeral. Because I would get used to filling myself up, and then I would have to go back to my usual hunger again. So I couldn't think of any way out except to die: I wanted death for myself sometimes just as much as for the others. But I never saw it, even though it was always inside of me.

Lots of times I thought about running away from that penny- pinching master, but I didn't for two reasons. First, I didn't trust my legs: lack of food had made them so skinny that I was afraid they wouldn't hold me up.

Second, I thought a while, and I said: "I've had two masters: the first one nearly starved me to death, and when I left him I met up with this one; and he gives me so little to eat that I've already got one foot in the grave. Well, if I leave this one and find a master who is one step lower, how could it possibly end except with my death?" So I didn't dare to move an inch. I really thought that each step would just get worse. And if I were to go down one more step, Lazaro wouldn't make another peep and no one would ever hear of him again.

So there I was, in a terrible state (and God help any true Christian who finds himself in those circumstances), not knowing what to do and seeing that I was going from bad to worse. Then one day when that miserable, tightfisted

master of mine had gone out, a tinker came to my door. I think he must have been an angel in disguise, sent down by the hand of God. He asked me if there was anything I wanted fixed. "You could fix me up, and you wouldn't be doing half bad," I said softly but not so he could hear me. But there wasn't enough time so I could waste it on witty sayings and, inspired by the Holy Spirit, I said to him, "Sir, I've lost the key to this chest, and I'm afraid my master will beat me. Please look and see if one of those keys you have will fit. I'll pay you for it."

The angelic tinker began to try out the keys on his chain, one after the other, and I was helping him with my feeble prayers. Then, when I least expected it, I saw the face of God, as they say, formed by the loaves of bread inside that chest. When it was all the way open I said to him, "I don't have any money to give you for the key, but take your payment from what's in there."

He took the loaf of bread that looked best to him, and he gave me the key and went away happy, leaving me even happier. But I didn't touch a thing right then so that the loss wouldn't be noticeable. And, too, when I saw that I was the Lord of all that, I didn't think my hunger would dare come near me. Then my miserly old master came back, and--thank God--he didn't notice the missing loaf of bread that the angel had carried off.

The next day, when he left the house, I opened my breadly paradise and sank my hands and teeth into a loaf, and in a flash I made it invisible. And, of course, I didn't forget to lock up the chest again. Then I began to sweep the house very happily, thinking that from now on my sad life would change. And so that day and the next I was happy. But it wasn't meant for that peace to last very long because on the third day real tertian fever struck.

It happened that I suddenly saw that man who was starving me to death standing over our chest, moving the loaves of bread from one side to the other, counting and recounting them. I pretended not to notice, and silently I was praying, hoping, and begging, "Saint John, blind him!" After he had stood there quite a while, counting the days and the loaves on his fingers, he said, "If I weren't so careful about keeping this chest closed, I'd swear that someone had taken some of the loaves of bread. But from now on, just to close the door on all suspicion, I'm going to keep close track of them. There are nine and a half in there now."

"May God send you nine pieces of bad news, too," I said under my breath. It seemed to me that what he said went into my heart like a hunter's arrow, and my stomach began to rumble when it saw that it would be going back to its old diet. Then he left the house. To console myself I opened the chest, and when I saw the bread I began to worship it--but I was afraid to "take any in remembrance of Him." Then I counted the loaves to see if the old miser had made a mistake, but he had counted them much better than I'd have liked. The best I could do was to kiss them over and over, and as delicately as I could, I peeled a little off the half-loaf on the side where it was already cut. And so I got through that day but not as happily as the one before.

But my hunger kept growing, mainly because my stomach had gotten used to more bread during those previous two or three days. I was dying a slow death, and finally I got to the point that when I was alone the only thing I did was open and close the chest and look at the face of God inside (or at least that's how children put it). But God Himself--who aids the afflicted-- seeing me in such straits, put a little thought into my head that would help me. Thinking to myself, I said: This chest is big and old, and it's got some holes in it, although they're small. But he might be led to believe that mice are getting into it and are eating the bread. It wouldn't do to take out a whole loaf: he'd notice that it was missing right away, since he hardly gives me any food at all to live on. But he'll believe this all right.

And I began to break off crumbs over some cheap tablecloths he had there. I would pick up one loaf and put another one down, so that I broke a few little pieces off of three or four of them. Then I ate those up just as if they were bonbons, and I felt a little better. But when he came home to eat and opened the chest, he saw the mess. And he really thought that mice had done the damage because I'd done my job to perfection, and it looked just like the work of mice. He looked the chest over from top to bottom, and he saw the holes where he suspected they'd gotten in. Then he called me over and said, "Lazaro, look! Look at what a terrible thing happened to our bread this evening!"

And I put on a very astonished face and asked him what it could have been.

"What else," he said, "but mice? They get into everything."

We began to eat, and--thank God--I came out all right in this, too. I got more bread than the miserable little bit he usually gave me because he sliced off the parts he thought the mice had chewed on, and said, "Eat this. The mouse is a very clean animal."

So that day, with the extra that I got by the work of my hands--or of my fingernails, to be exact--we finished our meal, although I never really got started.

And then I got another shock: I saw him walking around carefully, pulling nails out of the walls and looking for little pieces of wood. And he used these to board up all the holes in the old chest.

"Oh, Lord!" I said then. "What a life full of misery, trials, and bad luck we're born into! How short the pleasures of this hard life of ours are! Here I was, thinking that this pitiful little cure of mine would get me through this miserable situation, and I was happy, thinking I was doing pretty well. Then along came my bad luck and woke up this miser of a master of mine and made him even more careful than usual (and misers are hardly ever not careful). Now, by closing up the holes in the chest, he's closing the door to my happiness, too, and opening the one to my troubles."

That's what I kept sighing while my conscientious carpenter finished up his job with nails and little boards, and said, "Now, my dear treacherous mice, you'd better think about changing your ways. You won't get anywhere in this house."

As soon as he left, I went to see his work. And I found that he didn't leave a hole where even a mosquito could get into the sorry old chest. I opened it up with my useless key, without a hope of getting anything. And there I saw the two or three loaves that I'd started to eat and that my master thought the mice had chewed on, and I still got a little bit off of them by touching them very lightly like an expert swordsman.

Since necessity is the father of invention and I always had so much of it, day and night I kept thinking about how I was going to keep myself alive. And I think that hunger lit up my path to these black solutions: they say that hunger sharpens your wits and that stuffing yourself dulls them, and that's just the way it worked with me.

Well, while I was lying awake one night thinking about this--how I could manage to start using the chest again--I saw that my master was asleep: it was obvious from the snoring and loud wheezing he always made while he slept. I got up very, very quietly, and since during the day I had planned out what I would do and had left an old knife lying where I'd find it, I went over to the sorry-looking chest, and in the place where it looked most defenseless, I attacked it with the knife, using it like a boring tool.

It was really an old chest, and it had been around for so many years that it didn't have any strength or backbone left. It was so soft and worm-eaten that it gave in to me right away and let me put a good-sized hole in its side so I could relieve my own suffering. When I finished this, I opened the slashed-up chest very quietly, and feeling around and finding the cut-up loaf, I did the usual thing--what you've seen before.

Feeling a little better after that, I closed it up again and went back to my straw mat. I rest-ed there and even slept a while. But I didn't sleep very well, and I thought it was because I hadn't eaten enough. And that's what it must have been because at that time all the troubles of the King of France wouldn't have been able to keep me awake. The next day my master saw the damage that had been done to the bread along with the hole I'd made, and he began to swear at the mice and say, "How can this be? I've never even seen a mouse in this house until now!"

And I really think he must have been telling the truth. If there was one house in the whole country that by rights should have been free of mice, it was that one, because they don't usually stay where there's nothing to eat. He began to look around on the walls of the house again for nails and pieces of wood to keep them out. Then when night came and he was asleep, there I was on my feet with my knife in hand, and all the holes he plugged up during the day I unplugged at night.

That's how things went, me following him so quickly that this must be where the saying comes from: "Where one door is closed, another opens." Well, we seemed to be doing Penelope's work on the cloth because whatever he wove during the day I took apart at night. And after just a few days and nights we had the poor pantry box in such a shape that, if you really wanted to call it by its proper name, you'd have to call it an old piece of armor instead of a chest because of all the nails and tacks in it.

When he saw that his efforts weren't doing any good, he said, "This chest is so beat up and the wood in it is so old and thin that it wouldn't be able to stand up against any mouse. And it's getting in such bad shape that if we put up with it any longer it won't keep anything secure. The worst part of it is that even though it

doesn't keep things very safe, if I got rid of it I really wouldn't be able to get along without it, and I'd just end up having to pay three or four pieces of silver to get another one. The best thing that I can think of, since what I've tried so far hasn't done any good, is to set a trap inside the chest for those blasted mice."

Then he asked someone to lend him a mousetrap, and with the cheese rinds that he begged from the neighbors, the trap was kept set and ready inside the chest. And that really turned out to be a help to me. Even though I didn't require any frills for eating, I was still glad to get the cheese rinds that I took out of the mousetrap, and even at that I didn't stop the mouse from raiding the bread.

When he found that mice had been into the bread and eaten the cheese, but that not one of them had been caught, he swore a blue streak and asked his neighbors, "How could a mouse take cheese out of a trap, eat it, leave the trap sprung, and still not get caught?" The neighbors agreed that it couldn't be a mouse that was causing the trouble because it would have had to have gotten caught sooner or later. So one neighbor said to him, "I remember that there used to be a snake around your house--that must be who the culprit is. It only stands to reason: it's so long it can get the food, and even though the trap is sprung on it, it's not completely inside, so it can get out again."

Everyone agreed with what he'd said, and that really upset my master. From then on he didn't sleep so soundly. Whenever he heard even a worm moving around in the wood at night, he thought it was the snake gnawing on the chest. Then he would be up on his feet, and he'd grab a club that he kept by the head of the bed ever since they'd mentioned a snake to him, and he would really lay into that poor old chest, hoping to scare the snake away. He woke up the neighbors with all the noise he made, and he wouldn't let me sleep at all. He came up to my straw mat and turned it over and me with it, thinking that the snake had headed for me and gotten into the straw or inside my coat. Because they told him that at night these creatures look for some place that's warm and even get into babies' cribs and bite them. Most of the time I pretended to be asleep, and in the morning he would ask me, "Didn't you feel anything last night, son? I was right behind the snake, and I think it got into your bed: they're very cold-blooded creatures, and they try to find a place that's warm."

"I hope to God it doesn't bite me," I said. "I'm really scared of it."

He went around all excited and not able to sleep, so that--on my word of honor--the snake (a male one, of course) didn't dare go out chewing at night, or even go near the chest. But in the daytime, while he was at church or in town, I did my looting. And when he saw the damage and that he wasn't able to do anything about it, he wandered around at night--as I've said--like a spook.

I was afraid that in his wanderings he might stumble onto my key that I kept under the straw. So it seemed to me that the safest thing was to put it in my mouth at night. Because since I'd been with the blind man my mouth had gotten round like a purse, and I could hold twenty or thirty coppers in it--all in half-copper coins--and eat at the same time. If I hadn't been able to do that I couldn't have gotten hold of even a copper that the blasted blind man wouldn't have found: he was always searching every patch and seam on my clothes. Well, as I say, I put the key in my mouth every night, and I went to sleep without being afraid that the zombie master of mine would stumble onto it. But when trouble is going to strike, you can't do a thing to stop it.

The fates--or to be more exact, my sins--had it in store for me that one night while I was sleeping my mouth must have been open, and the key shifted so that the air I breathed out while I was asleep went through the hollow part of the key. It was tubular, and (unfortunately for me) it whistled so loud that my master heard it and got excited. He must have thought it was the snake hissing, and I guess it really sounded like one.

He got up very quietly with his club in hand, and by feeling his way toward the sound he came up to me very softly so the snake wouldn't hear him. And when he found himself so close, he thought that it had come over to where I was lying, looking for a warm place, and had slipped into the straw. So, lifting the club up high, and thinking that he had the snake trapped down there and that he would hit it so hard that he'd kill it, he swung down on me with such a mighty blow that he knocked me unconscious and left my head bashed in.

Then he saw that he'd hit me (I must have really cried out when the blow leveled me), and--as he later told me--he reached over and shouted at me, calling my name and trying to revive me.

But when his hands touched me and he felt all the blood, he realized what he'd done, and he went off to get a light right away. When he came back with it he found me moaning with the key still in my mouth: I had never let loose of it, and it was still sticking half out--just like it must have been when I was whistling through it.

The snake killer was terrified, wondering what it could be. He took it all the way out of my mouth and looked at it. Then he realized what it was because its ridges matched his key exactly. He went to try it out, and he solved the crime. Then that cruel hunter must have said: "I've found the mouse and the snake that were fighting me and eating me out of house and home."

I can't say for sure what happened during the next three days because I spent them inside the belly of the whale. But what I've just told I heard about from my master when I came to; he was telling what had happened in detail to everyone who came by. At the end of three days, when I was back in my senses, I found myself stretched out on my straw bed with my head all bandaged up and full of oils and salves. And I got scared and said, "What is this?"

The cruel priest answered, "It seems that I caught the mice and snakes that were ruining me."

I looked myself over, and when I saw how badly beaten up I was, I guessed what had happened.

Then an old lady who was a healer came in, along with the neighbors. And they began to take the wrappings off my head and treat the wound. When they saw that I was conscious again, they were very happy, and they said, 'Well, he's got his senses back. God willing, it won't be too serious."

Then they began to talk again about what had happened to me and to laugh. While I--

sinner that I am--I was crying. Anyway, they fed me, and I was famished, but they really didn't give me enough. Yet, little by little, I recovered, and two weeks later I was able to get up, out of any danger (but not out of my state of hunger) and nearly cured.

The next day when I'd gotten up, my master took me by the hand and led me out the door, and when I was in the street he said to me: "Lazaro, from now on you're on your own--I don't want you. Go get yourself another master, and God be with you. I don't want such a diligent servant here with me. You could only have become this way from being a blind man's guide."

Then he crossed himself as if I had the devil in me and went back into his house and closed the door.

III - How Lazaro Took up with a Squire and What Happened to Him Then

So I had to push on ahead, as weak as I was. And little by little, with the help of some good people, I ended up in this great city of Toledo. And here, by the grace of God, my wounds healed in about two weeks. People were always giving me things while I was hurt, but when I was well again, they told me, "You-- you're nothing but a lazy, no-good sponger. Go on--go find yourself a good master you can work for."

"And where will I meet up with one of those," I said to myself, "unless God makes him from scratch, the way he created the world?"

While I was going along begging from door to door (without much success, since charity seemed to have gone up to heaven), God had me run into a squire who was walking down the street. He was well dressed, his hair was combed, and he walked and looked like a real gentleman. I looked at him, and he looked at me, and he said, "Boy, are you looking for a master?"

And I said, "Yes, sir."

"Well, come with me," he said. "God has been good to you, making you run into me. You

must have been doing some good praying today."

So I went with him. And I thanked God
that he asked me to go along because--with his
nice-looking clothes and the way he looked--I
thought he was just what I needed.

It was morning when I found my third
master. And I followed him through most of the
city. We went through squares where they were
selling bread and different things. And I was

hoping and praying that he would load me up with some of the food they were selling because it was just the right time for shopping. But very quickly, without stopping, we went right past those places. Maybe he doesn't like what he sees here, I thought, and he wants to buy his groceries somewhere else.

So we kept on walking until it was eleven o'clock. Then he went into the cathedral, and I was right behind him. I saw him listen to mass and go through the other holy ceremonies very devoutly, until it was over and the people had gone. Then we came out of the church.

We began to go down a street at a good clip. And I was the happiest fellow in the world, since we hadn't stopped to buy any food. I really thought my new master was one of those people who do all their shopping at once, and that our meal would be there, ready and waiting for us, just the way I wanted--and, in fact, the way I needed.

At that minute the clock struck one--an hour past noon--and we came to a house where my master stopped, and so did I. And pulling his cape to the left, he took a key out of his sleeve and opened the door, and we both went into the house. The entrance was dark and gloomy: it looked like it would make anyone who went in afraid. But inside there was a little patio and some fairly nice rooms.

Once we were in, he took off his cape: he asked me if my hands were clean, and then we shook it out and folded it. And blowing the dust very carefully off a stone bench that was there, he put the cape down on top of it. And when that was done, he sat down next to it and asked me a lot of questions about where I was from and how I'd happened to come to that city.

I talked about myself longer than I wanted to because I thought it was more a time to have the table set and the stew dished up than to tell him about all that. Still, I satisfied him about myself, lying as well as I could. I told him all my good points but kept quiet about the rest, since I didn't think that was the time for them. When that was over, he just sat there for a while. I began to realize that that was a bad sign, since it was almost two o'clock and I hadn't seen him show any more desire to eat than a dead man.

Then I began to think about his keeping the door locked, and the fact that I hadn't heard any other sign of life in the whole house. The only thing I'd seen were walls: not a chair, not a meat-cutting board, a stool, a table, or even a chest like the one I'd had before. And I began to wonder if that house was under a spell. While I was thinking about this, he said to me, "Boy, have you eaten?"

"No, sir," I said. "It wasn't even eight o'clock when I met you."

"Well, even though it was still morning, I'd already had breakfast. And when I eat like that, I want you to know that I'm satisfied until nighttime. So you'll just have to get along as well as you can: we'll have supper later."

You can see how, when I heard this, I nearly dropped in my tracks--not so much from hunger but because fate seemed to be going completely against me. Then all my troubles passed before my eyes again, and I began to cry over my hardships once more. I remembered my reasoning when I was thinking about leaving the priest: I figured that even though he was mean and stingy, it might turn out that I would meet up with someone worse. So there I was, moping over the hard life I'd had and over my death that was getting nearer and nearer.

And yet, keeping back my emotions as well as I could, I said to him, "Sir, I am only a boy, and thank God I'm not too concerned about eating. I can tell you that I was the lightest eater of all my friends, and all the masters I've ever had have praised that about me right up to now."

"That really is a virtue," he said, "and it makes me appreciate you even more. Because only pigs stuff themselves: gentlemen eat moderately."

I get the picture! I thought to myself. Well, damn all the health and virtue that these masters I run into find in staying hungry.

I went over next to the door and took out of my shirt some pieces of bread that I still had from begging. When he saw this, he said to me, "Come here, boy. What are you eating?"

I went over to him and showed him the bread. There were three pieces, and he took one--the biggest and best one. Then he said, "Well, well, this does look like good bread."

"It is!" I said. "But tell me, sir, do you really think so now?"

"Yes, I do," he said. "Where did you get it? I wonder if the baker had clean hands?"

"I can't tell you that," I said, but it certainly doesn't taste bad."

"Let's see if you're right," said my poor master.

And he put it in his mouth and began to gobble it down as ferociously as I was doing with mine.

"Bless me, this bread is absolutely delicious," he said.

When I saw what tree he was barking up, I began to eat faster. Because I realized that if he finished before I did, he would be nice enough to help me with what was left. So we finished almost at the same time. And he began to brush off a few crumbs--very tiny ones--that were left on his shirt. Then he went into a little room nearby and brought out a chipped-up jug--not a very new one--and after he had drunk, he offered it to me. But, so I would look like a teetotaler, I said, "Sir, I don't drink wine."

"It's water," he said. "You can drink that."

Then I took the jug, and I drank. But not much, because being thirsty wasn't exactly my trouble. So that's how we spent the day until nighttime: him asking me questions and me answering as best I could. Then he took me to the room where the jug that we'd drunk from was, and he said to me, "Boy, get over there, and I'll show you how this bed is made up so that you'll be able to do it from now on."

I went down to one end, and he went over to the other, and we made up the blasted bed. There really wasn't much to do: it just had a bamboo frame sitting on some benches, and on top of that there was a filthy mattress with the bedclothes stretched over it. And since it hadn't been washed very often, it really didn't look much like a mattress. But that's what it was used for, though there was a lot less stuffing than it needed. We stretched it out and tried to soften it up. But that was impossible because you can't make a really hard object soft. And that blessed packsaddle had hardly a damned thing inside of it. When it was put on the frame, every strut showed through, and it looked just like the rib cage of a real skinny pig. And on top of that starving pad he put a cover of the same stamp: I never could decide what color it was. With the bed made and night on us, he said to me, "Lazaro, it's late now, and it's a long way from here to the square. And besides, there are a lot of thieves who go around stealing at night in this city. Let's get along as well as we can, and tomorrow, when it's daytime, God will be good to us. I've been living alone, and so I haven't stocked up any groceries: instead, I've been eating out. But from now on we'll do things differently."

"Sir," I said, "don't worry about me. I can spend one night--or more, if I have to--without eating."

"You'll live longer and you'll be healthier too," he answered. "Because as we were saying today, there's nothing in the world like eating moderately to live a long life."

If that's the way things are, I thought to myself, I never will die. Because I've always been forced to keep that rule, and with my luck I'll probably keep it all my life.

And he lay down on the bed, using his pants and jacket as a pillow. He told me to stretch out at his feet, so I did. But I didn't get a damned bit of sleep! The frame struts and my protruding bones didn't stop squabbling and fighting all night long. With all the pains, hunger, and trouble I'd been through, I don't think there was a pound of flesh left on my body. And since I'd hardly had a bite to eat that day, I was groveling in hunger--and hunger and sleep don't exactly make good bedfellows. So I cursed myself (God forgive me!) and my bad luck over and over, nearly all night long. And what was worse, I didn't dare to turn over because I might wake him up. So I just kept asking God for death.

When morning came we got up, and he began to shake out and clean his pants and jacket and his coat and cape (while I stood around like an idle servant!). And he took his own good time about getting dressed. I brought some water for him to wash his hands, and then he combed his hair and put his sword in the belt, and while he was doing that, he said: "If you only knew what a prize this is, boy! I wouldn't sell it for any amount of money in the world. And I'll have you know that of all the swords the famous Toledan swordmaker Antonio made, there isn't one that he put as sharp an edge on as this one has."

And he pulled it out of the sheath and felt it with his fingers and said, "Look here. I'll bet I could slice a ball of wool with it." And I thought to myself: And with my teeth--even though they're not made of steel--I could slice a four-pound loaf of bread.

He put it back in the sheath and strapped it on, and then he hung a string of large beads from the sword belt. And he walked slowly, holding his body straight and swaying gracefully as he walked. And every so often he would put the tail of the cape over his shoulder or under his arm. And with his right hand on his side, he went out the door, saying, "Lazaro, while I go to mass, you watch the house. Make the bed and fill the pitcher up with water from the river just down below us. Be sure to lock the door so that nothing will get stolen, and put the key on the

hinge here so that if I come back while you're
gone I can get in."

Then he went up the street with such a
stately expression and manner that anyone who
didn't know him would think he was a close relative to the Count of Arcos, or at least his valet.

I stood there, thinking: "Bless You, Lord--
You give us sickness and You cure us too! My
master looks so content that anyone who saw
him would think he'd eaten a huge supper last

night and slept in a nice bed. And even though it's early in the morning, they'd think he'd had a good breakfast. Your ways are mighty mysterious, Lord, and people don't understand them! With that refined way he acts and that nice-looking cape and coat he'd fool anyone. And who would believe that that gracious man got by all day yesterday on a piece of bread that his servant Lazaro had carried all day and night inside his shirt for safekeeping--not really the most sanitary place in the world--and that today when he washed his hands and face, he dried them on his shirttail because we didn't have any towels? Nobody would suspect it, of course. Oh Lord, how many of these people do You have scattered around the world who suffer for the filth that they call honor what they would never suffer for You!"

So I stood at the door, thinking about these things and looking until my master had disappeared down the long, narrow street. Then I went back into the house, and in a second I walked through the whole place, both upstairs and down, without stopping or finding anything to stop for. I made up that blasted hard bed and took the jug down to the river. And I saw my master in a garden, trying hard to coax two veiled women--they looked like the kind that are always hanging around that place. In fact, a lot of them go there in the summer to take the early morning air. And they go down to those cool riverbanks to eat breakfast-- without even bringing any food along; they're sure someone will give them some, since the men around there have got them in the habit of doing that.

As I say, there he was with them just like the troubador Macias, telling them more sweet words than Ovid ever wrote. And when they saw that he was pretty well softened up, they weren't ashamed to ask him for some breakfast, promising the usual payment.

But his pocketbook was as cold as his stomach was warm, and he began to have such hot chills that the color drained from his face, and he started to trip over his tongue and make up some lame excuses.

They must have been pretty experienced women because they caught on to his illness right away and left him there for what he was.

I'd been eating some cabbage stalks, and that was my breakfast. And since I was a new servant, I went back home very diligently without my master seeing me. I decided I'd sweep out a little there, since that's what the place really needed, but I couldn't find anything to sweep with. Then I began to think about what I should do, and I decided to wait until noon for my master because if he came he might bring something to eat; but that turned out to be a waste of time.

When I saw that it was getting to be two o'clock and he still hadn't come, I began to be attacked by hunger. So I locked the door and put the key where he told me to, and then I went back to my old trade. With a low, sickly voice,

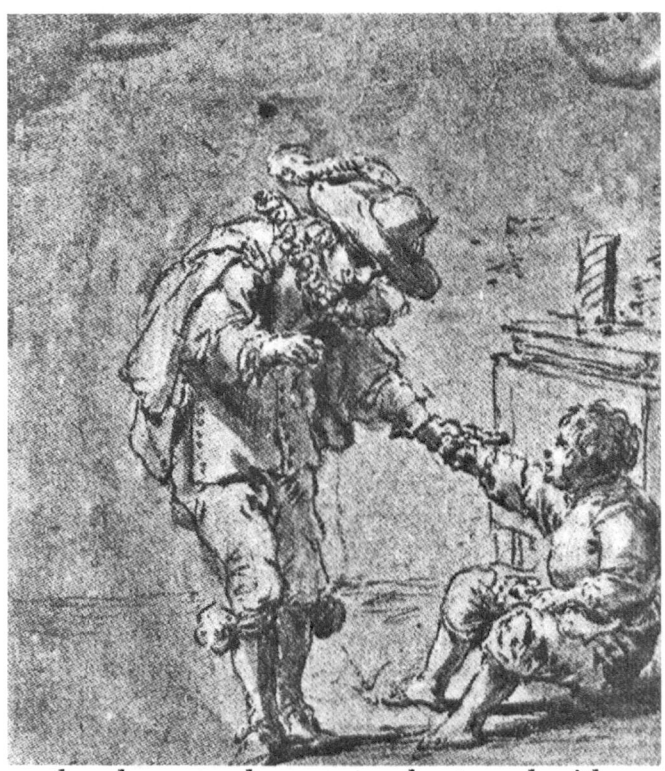

my hands crossed over my chest, and with my eyes looking up to heaven and God's name on my tongue, I began to beg for bread at the doors of the biggest houses I saw. But I'd been doing this almost from the cradle--I mean I learned it from that great teacher, the blind man, and I turned out to be a pretty good student--so even though this town had never been very charitable, and it had been a pretty lean year besides, I handled myself so well that before the clock struck four I had that many pounds of bread stored away in my stomach and at least two more in my sleeves and inside my shirt.

I went back to the house, and on my way through the meat market I begged from one of the women there, and she gave me a piece of cow's hoof along with some cooked tripe.

When I got home my good master was there, his cape folded and lying on the stone bench, and he was walking around in the patio. I went inside, and he came over to me. I thought he was going to scold me for being late, but God had something better in store. He asked me where I'd been, and I told him, "Sir, I was here until two o'clock, and when I saw that you weren't coming, I went to the city and put myself in the hands of the good people there, and they gave me what you see here."

I showed him the bread and the tripe that I was carrying in my shirttail, and his face lit up, and he said: 'Well, I held up dinner for you, but when I saw that you weren't going to come, I went ahead and ate. But what you've done there is all right because it's better to beg in God's name than it is to steal. That's my opinion, so help me. The only thing I ask is that you don't tell anyone that you're living with me because it will hurt my honor. But I think it would stay a secret anyway, since hardly anyone in this town knows me. I wish I'd never come here!"

"Don't worry about that, sir," I said. "No one would give a damn about asking me that, and I wouldn't tell them even if they did."

"Well then, eat, you poor sinner. If it's God's will, we'll soon see ourselves out of these straits. But I want you to know that ever since I came to this house nothing has gone right for me. There must be an evil spell on it. You know there are some unlucky houses that are cursed, and the bad luck rubs off on the people who live in them. I don't doubt for a minute that this is one of them, but I tell you that after this month is over, I wouldn't live here even if they gave the place to me."

I sat down at the end of the stone bench, and I kept quiet about my snack so that he wouldn't take me for a glutton. So, for supper I began to eat my tripe and bread, while I was watching my poor master out of the corner of my eye. And he kept staring at my shirttail that I was using for a plate. I hope God takes as much pity on me as I felt for him. I knew just what he was feeling, since the same thing had happened to me lots of times-- and, in fact, it was still happening to me. I thought about asking him to join me, but since he told me that he'd already eaten I was afraid he wouldn't accept the invitation. The fact is, I was hoping that the sinner would help himself to the food I had gone to the trouble of getting and that he'd eat the way he did the day before so he could get out of his own troubles. This was really a better time for it, since there was more food and I wasn't as hungry.

God decided to grant my wish--and his, too, I guess. Because he was still walking around, but when I began to eat, he came over to me and said, "I tell you, Lazaro, I've never seen anyone eat with as much gusto as you put into it. Anyone watching you would get hungry on the spot, even if he hadn't been before."

The marvelous appetite you have, I thought to myself, makes you think mine is beautiful.

Still, I decided to help him, since he had opened up a way for me himself. So I said to him, "Sir, a man can do a good job if he has good tools. This bread is absolutely delicious, and the cow's hoof is so well cooked and seasoned that no one could possibly resist its taste."

"Is it cow's hoof?"

"Yes, sir."

"I tell you, there's no better dish in the world. I don't even like pheasant as much."

"Well, dig in, sir, and you'll see how good it really is."

71

I put the cow's hooves into his, along with three or four of the whiter pieces of bread. And he sat down beside me and began to eat like a man who was really hungry. He chewed the meat off of every little bone better than any hound of his would have done.

"With garlic sauce," he said, "this is an exceptional dish."

"You don't need any sauce with your appetite," I said under my breath.

"By God, that tasted so good you'd think I hadn't had a bite to eat all day."

That's true as sure as I was born, I said to myself.

He asked me for the water jug, and when I gave it to him it was as full as when I'd first brought it in. Since there was no water gone from it, there was a sure sign that my master hadn't been overeating that day. We drank and went to sleep, very content, like we'd done the night before.

Well, to make a long story short, that's the way we spent the next nine or ten days: that sinner would go out in the morning with his satisfied, leisurely pace, to dawdle around the streets while I was out hoofing it for him.

I used to think lots of times about my catastrophe: having escaped from those terrible masters I'd had and looking for someone better, I ran into a man who not only couldn't support me but who I had to support. Still, I really liked him because I saw that he didn't have anything and he couldn't do more than he was already doing. I felt more sorry for him than angry. And lots of times, just so I could bring back something for him to eat, I didn't eat anything myself.

I did this because one morning the pitiful fellow got up in his shirt and went to the top floor of the house to take care of a certain necessity. And to satisfy my curiosity I unfolded the jacket and pants he'd left at the head of the bed. And I found an old, crumpled-up little purse of satiny velvet that didn't have a damned cent in it, and there wasn't any sign that it had had one for a long time.

"This man," I said, "is poor. And no one can give what he doesn't have. But both the stingy blind man and that blasted miser of a priest did all right in God's name--one of them with a quick tongue and the other one with his hand-kissing. And they were starving me to death. So it's only right that I should hate them and feel sorry for this man."

As God is my witness, even today when I run into someone like him, with that pompous way of walking of his, I feel sorry for them because I think that they may be suffering what I saw this one go through. But even with all his poverty, I'd still be glad to serve him more than the others because of the things I've just mentioned. There was only one little thing that I didn't like about him: I wished that he wouldn't act so superior; if only he'd let his vanity come down a little to be in line with his growing necessity. But it seems to me that that's a rule his kind always keeps: even if they don't have a red cent to their name, they have to keep up the masquerade. God help them or that's the way they'll go to their graves.

Well, while I was there, getting along the way I said, my bad luck (which never got tired of haunting me) decided that that hard, foul way of life shouldn't last. The way it happened was that, since there had been a crop failure there that year, the town council decided to make all the beggars who came from other towns get out of the city. And they announced that from then on if they found one of them there, he'd be whipped. So the law went into effect, and four days after the announcement was given I saw a procession of beggars being led through the streets and whipped. And I got so scared that I didn't dare go out begging any more.

It's not hard to imagine the dieting that went on in my house and the sadness and silence of the people living there. It was so bad that for two or three days at a time we wouldn't have a bite to eat or even say one word to each other. I knew some ladies who lived next door to us; they spun cotton and made hats, and they kept me alive. From what little they brought in they always gave me something, and I just about managed to get by.

But I didn't feel as sorry for myself as I did for my poor master: he didn't have a damned bite to eat in a week. At least, we didn't have anything to eat at the house. When he went out I don't know how he got along, where he went or what he ate. And if you could only have seen him coming down the street at noon, holding himself straight, and skinnier than a full-blooded greyhound! And because of his damn what-do-you-call it--honor-- he would take a toothpick (and there weren't very many of those in the house either) and go out the door, picking at what didn't have anything between them and still grumbling about the cursed place. He'd say, "Look how bad things are. And it's this blasted house that's causing it all. Look how gloomy and dark and dismal it is. As long as we stay here, we're going to suffer. I wish the month were over so we could get out of here."

Well, while we were in this terrible, hungry state, one day--I don't know by what stroke of luck or good fortune--a silver piece found its way into the poor hands of my master. And he brought it home with him, looking as proud as if he had all the money in Venice, and smiling very happily, he gave it to me and said: "Take this, Lazaro. God is beginning to be good to us. Go down to the square and buy bread and wine and meat. Let's shoot the works! And also--this should make you happy--I want you to know that I've rented another house, so we'll only stay in this unlucky place until the end of the month. Damn the place and damn the person who put the first tile on its roof-- I should never have rented it. I swear to God that as long as I've lived here I haven't had a drop of wine or a bite of meat, and I haven't gotten any rest. And it's all because of the way this place looks--so dark and gloomy! Go on now, and come back as quick as you can: we'll eat like kings today."

I took my silver coin and my jug, and hurrying along, I went up the street, heading for the square, very content and happy. But what's the use if my bad luck has it planned for me that I can't enjoy anything without trouble coming along with it? And that's the way this thing went. I was going up the street, thinking about how I would spend the money in the best way possible and get the most out of it. And I was thanking God with all my heart for letting my master have some money, when suddenly I came upon a corpse that a bunch of clergy and other people were carrying down the street on a litter.

I squeezed up next to the wall to let them by, and after the body had gone past there came right behind the litter a woman who must have been the dead man's wife, all dressed up in

mourning (and a lot of other women with her).
And she came along, crying loudly and saying,
"My husband and lord, where are they taking
you? It's to that poor, unhappy house, that dark
and gloomy house, that house where they never
eat or drink!"

And when I heard that, I felt like I had
fallen through the ground, and I said, "Oh--no!
They're taking this dead man to my house."

I turned around and squeezed through
the crowd and ran back down the street as fast as
I could toward my house. And when I got inside
I closed the door right behind me and called out

for my master to come and help me. And I grabbed hold of him and begged him to help me block the door. He was a little stunned, thinking it might be something else, and he asked me, "What is it, boy? Why are you shouting? What's the matter? Why did you slam the door so hard?"

"Oh, sir," I said, "help me! They're bringing a dead man here."

"What do you mean?" he asked.

"I stumbled into him just up the way from here, and his wife was coming along saying, 'My husband and lord, where are they taking you? To the dark and gloomy house, the poor, unhappy house, the house where they never eat or drink!' Oh, sir, they're bringing him here."

And I tell you that when my master heard that, even though he didn't have any reason for being very cheerful, he laughed so hard that for a long time he couldn't even talk. In the meantime I had the bolt snapped shut on the door and my shoulder against it to hold them all back. The people passed by with their corpse, and I was still afraid that they were going to stick him in our house. And when he'd had his bellyful of laughter (more than of food) my good master said to me: "It's true, Lazaro, that taking the words of the widow at face value, you had every reason to think what you did. But since it was God's will to do something else and they've gone by, go on and open the door and go get us something to eat."

"Sir, wait until they've gone down the street," I said.

Finally my master came up to the door that led to the street and opened it, reassuring me--and I really needed that because I was so upset and afraid. So I started up the street again.

But even though we ate well that day, I didn't enjoy it a damn bit. In fact, I didn't get my color back for three days. And my master would grin every time he thought about what I'd done.

So that's what happened to me during those days with my third poor master, this squire, and all the time I was wishing I knew how he'd come to this place and why he was staying here. Because from the very first day that I started serving him, I realized he was a stranger here: he hardly knew anyone, and he didn't associate with very many of the people around here.

Finally my wish came true, and I found out what I wanted to know. One day after we'd eaten fairly well and he was pretty content, he told me about himself. He said he was from Old Castile. And he said the only reason he'd left there was because he didn't want to take his hat off to a neighbor of his who was a high- class gentleman.

"Sir," I said, "if he was the kind of man you say he was and his status was higher than yours, it was only right for you to take your hat off first--after all, you say that he took off his hat, too."

"That is the kind of man he was: his status was higher and he did take his hat off to me. But considering all the time I took mine off first, it wouldn't have been asking too much for him to be civil and make the first move once in a while."

"It seems to me, sir," I told him, "that I wouldn't even think about that--especially with people who are my superiors and are better off than I am."

"You're just a boy," he answered, "and you don't understand honor. That is the most important thing to any self-respecting gentleman these days. Well, I want you to know that I'm a squire--as you can see. But I swear to God that if I meet a count on the street and he doesn't take his hat all the way off his head for me, the next time I see him coming, I'll duck right into a house and pretend that I have some business or other to do there. Or I'll go up another street, if there is one, before he gets up to me--just so I won't have to take off my hat to him. Because a gentleman doesn't owe anything to anyone except God or the King. And it isn't right, if he's a man of honor, for him to let his self-respect fall even for a minute.

"I remember one day when I put a craftsman from my town in his place, and I felt like strangling him, too, because every time I ran into him he would say, 'God keep you, friend.' 'You little peasant,' I said to him, 'How dare you address me with "God keep you" as if I were just anybody? Where were you brought up?' And from that day on, whenever he saw me, he took off his hat and spoke to me the way he was supposed to."

"But isn't that a good way for one man to greet another: to say 'God keep you'?"

"Damn it!" he said. "That's what they say to the lower classes. But to people who are higher up, like me, they're only supposed to say, 'I hope you are well today, sir.' Or, at least, 'I hope you feel well today' if the person talking to me is a gentleman. So I didn't want to put up with that man from my town who was filling me up to here with his 'God keep you.' And I wouldn't put up with him either. In fact, I won't stand for anyone--including the King himself--to say to me 'God keep you, friend.'"

"Well, I'll be...," I said. "That's why God doesn't help you out. You won't let anyone ask Him to."

"Especially," he said, "because I'm not so poor. In fact, where I'm from I have a huge estate (it's fifty miles from where I was born, right along Costanilla, the main street of Valladolid). And if the houses on it were still standing and kept up, it would be worth more than six thousand pieces of silver--just to give you an idea of how big and grand it would be. And I have a pigeon house that would produce more than two hundred pigeons a year if it hadn't fallen down. And there are some other things I won't mention, but I left them all because of my honor.

"And I came to this city, thinking I'd find a good position. But it hasn't turned out the way I thought it would. I meet lots of canons and other officials of the church, but those people are so tight with their money that no one could possibly get them to change their ways. Lesser men want me, too, but working for them is a lot of trouble. They want you to change from a man into a jack-of-all-trades, and if you won't, they give you the sack. And, generally, the paydays are few and far between; most of the time your only sure way of being paid is when they feed you. And when they want to have a clear conscience and really pay you for the sweat of your brow, your payoff comes from their clothes closet with a sweaty old jacket or a ragged cape or coat. And even when a man has a position with someone of the nobility, he still has his troubles.

"I ask you: aren't I clever enough to serve one of them and make him happy? Lord, if I ran into one, I really think I'd be his favorite--and I could do lots of things for him. Why, I could lie to him just as well as anyone else could. And I could flatter him like nothing he'd ever seen before. And I'd laugh at his stories and jokes even if they weren't exactly the funniest things in the world. I'd never tell him anything disturbing even if he would be better off knowing it. I would be very conscientious in everything about him, both in word and in deed. And I wouldn't kill myself to do things he wouldn't see. Whenever he was around to hear me, I would always scold the servants so he'd think I was very concerned about him. And if he were scolding one of his servants, I'd step in with some pointed remarks about the culprit that would make the nobleman even madder, while I was appearing to take the servant's side. I would praise the things he liked, but I'd mock and slander the people of the house and even the ones who didn't live there. I would go prying and try to find out about other people's lives so I could tell him about them.

"And I'd do all sorts of other things like this that go on in palaces these days and that people in that sort of a position like. They don't want to see good men in their homes. In fact, they think they're useless, and actually, they hate them. They say they're stupid people you can't deal with and that a nobleman can't confide in them. And smart people these days act with the nobility, as I say, just the way I would. But with my bad luck, I haven't met one of them."

And so my master complained about his unhappy life, too, telling me how admirable he was.

Well, about this time, a man and an old woman came in the door. The man wanted the rent money for the house, and the old lady had rented him the bed and wanted the money for that. They figured up the amount, and for two months' rent they wanted what he couldn't have made in a year. I think it was about twelve or thirteen pieces of silver. And he answered them very courteously: he said that he would go out to the square to change a doubloon and that they should come back that afternoon. But when he left, he never came back.

So they returned in the afternoon, but it was too late. I told them that he still hadn't come back. And when night came and he didn't, I was afraid to stay in the house alone. So I went to the women next door and told them what had happened, and I slept at their place.

The next morning, the creditors returned. But no one was home, so they came to the door of the place I was staying at now and asked about their neighbor. And the women told them, "Here is his servant and the door key."

Then they asked me about him, and I told them I didn't know where he was and that he hadn't come back home after going to get the change. And I said that I thought he'd given both them and me the slip.

When they heard that, they went to get a constable and a notary. And then they came back with them and took the key and called me and some witnesses over. And they opened the door and went inside to take my master's property until he paid what he owed them. They walked through the entire house and found it empty, just as I've said. And they asked me, "What's become of your master's things--his chests and drapes and furniture?"

"I don't know anything about that," I answered.

"It's obvious," they said, "that last night they must have had it all taken out and carted somewhere else. Constable, arrest this boy. He knows where it is."

Then the constable came over and grabbed me by the collar of my jacket, and he said, "Boy, you're under arrest unless you tell us what's happened to your master's things."

I'd never seen myself in such a fix (I had, of course, been held by the collar lots of times before, but that was done gently so that I could guide that man who couldn't see down the road), and so I was really scared. And while crying, I promised to answer their questions.

"All right," they said. "Then tell us what you know. Don't be afraid."

The notary sat down on a stone bench so he could write out the inventory, and he asked me what things my master had.

"Sir," I said, "according to what my master told me, he has a nice estate with houses on it and a pigeon house that isn't standing any more."

"All right," they said. "Even though it probably isn't worth much, it will be enough to pay off his bill. And what part of the city is it located in?" they asked me.

"In his town," I answered.

"For God's sake, we're really getting far," they said. "And just where is his town?"

"He told me that he came from Old Castile," I replied.

And the constable and notary laughed out loud, and said, "This sort of information would be good enough to pay off your debt even if it was bigger."

The neighbor ladies were there, and they said: "Gentlemen, this is just an innocent boy, and he's only been with that squire a few days. He doesn't know any more about him than you do. Besides, the poor little fellow has been coming to our house, and we've given him what we could to eat out of charity, and at night he's gone to his master's place to sleep."

When they saw that I was innocent, they let me loose and said I was free to go. And the constable and notary wanted the man and the woman to pay them for their services. And there was a lot of shouting and arguing about that. They said they weren't obligated to pay: there was no reason for them to, since nothing had been attached. But the men said that they had missed out on some other more profitable business just so they could come here.

Finally, after a lot of shouting, they loaded the old lady's old mattress onto a deputy-- even though it wasn't very much of a load. And all five of them went off, shouting at each other. I don't know how it all turned out. I think that sinner of a mattress must have paid everyone's expenses. And that was a good use for it because the time it should have spent relaxing and resting from its past strain, it had still been going around being rented out.

So, as I've said, my poor third master left me, and I saw the hand of my bad luck in this, too. It showed how much it was going against me, because it arranged my affairs so backward that instead of me leaving my master--which is what normally happens-- my master left and ran away from me.

IV - How Lazaro Went to Work for a Friar of the Order of Mercy and What Happened to Him

I had to get a fourth master, and this one turned out to be a friar of the Order of Mercy. The women I've mentioned recommended me to him. They said he was a relative. He didn't think much of choir duties or eating in the monastery; he was always running around on the outside; and he was really devoted to secular business and visiting. In fact, he was so dedicated to this that I think he wore out more shoes than the whole monastery put together. He gave me the first pair of shoes I ever wore, but they didn't last me a week. And I wouldn't have lasted much longer myself trying to keep up with him. So because of this and some other little things that I don't want to mention, I left him.

V - *How Lazaro Went to Work for a Pardoner and the Things That Happened to Him Then*

As luck would have it, the fifth one I ran into was a seller of papal indulgences. He was arrogant, without principles, the biggest hawker of indulgences that I've ever seen in my life or ever hope to see--and probably the biggest one of all time. He had all sorts of ruses and under-handed tricks, and he was always thinking up new ones.

When he'd come to a place where he was going to sell these pardons, first he'd give the priests and the other clergy some presents--just little things that really weren't worth much: some lettuce from Murcia; a couple limes or or-anges if they were in season; maybe a peach; some pears--the kind that stay green even after they're ripe. That way he tried to win them over so they'd look kindly on his business and call out their congregation to buy up the indulgences.

When they thanked him, he'd find out how well educated they were. If they said they understood Latin, he wouldn't speak a word of it so they couldn't trip him up; instead he'd use some refined, polished-sounding words and flowery phrases. And if he saw that these clerics were "appointed reverends"--I mean that they bought their way into the priesthood instead of by going through school- -he turned into a Saint Thomas, and for two hours he'd speak Latin. Or, at least, something that sounded like Latin even if it wasn't.

When they wouldn't take his pardons willingly, he'd try to find some underhanded way to get them to take them. To do that, he'd sometimes make a nuisance of himself, and other times he'd use his bag of tricks. It would take too long to talk about all the things I saw him do, so I'll just tell about one that was really sly and clever, and I think that will show how good he was at it.

In a place called Sagra, in the province of Toledo, he'd been preaching for two or three days, trying his usual gimmicks, and not one person had bought an indulgence, and I couldn't see that they had any intention of buying any. He swore up and down, and trying to think of what to do, he decided to call the town together the next morning so he could try to sell all the pardons.

And that night, after supper, he and the constable began to gamble to see who would pay for the meal. They got to quarreling over the game, and there were heated words. He called the constable a thief, and the constable called him a swindler. At that point my master, the pardoner, picked up a spear that was lying against the door of the room where they were playing. The constable reached for his sword, that he kept at his side.

The guests and neighbors came running at the noise and shouting we all began to make, and they got in between the two of them to break it up. Both men were really mad, and they tried to get away from the people who were holding them back so they could kill each other. But since those people had come swarming in at all the noise, the house was full of them, and when the two men saw that they couldn't use their weapons they began to call each other names. And at one point the constable said my master was a swindler and that all the pardons he was selling were counterfeit.

Finally, the townspeople saw that they couldn't make them stop, so they decided to get the constable out of the inn and take him somewhere else. And that made my master even madder. But after the guests and neighbors pleaded with him to forget about it and go home to bed he left, and then so did everyone else.

The next morning my master went to the church and told them to ring for mass so he could preach and sell the indulgences. And the townspeople came, muttering about the pardons, saying that they were forgeries and that the constable himself had let it out while they were quarreling. So, if they hadn't wanted to take any pardons before, they were dead set against it now.

The pardoner went up to the pulpit and began his sermon, trying to stir up the people, telling them that they shouldn't be without the blessings and the forgiveness that would come to them by buying the indulgences.

When he was into the sermon in full swing, the constable came in the church door, and after praying he got up, and with a loud and steady voice he began to speak very solemnly: "My fellow men, let me say a word; afterward, you can listen to whoever you like. I came here with this swindler who's preaching. But he tricked me: he said that if I helped him in his business, we'd split the profits. And now, seeing how it would hurt my conscience and your pocketbooks, I've repented of what I've done. And I want to tell you openly that the indulgences he's selling are forgeries. Don't believe him and don't buy them. I'm not involved with them any longer--either in an open or a hidden way--and from now on I'm giving up my staff, the symbol of my office, and I throw it on the ground so that you'll see I mean it. And if sometime in the future this man is punished for his cheating, I want you to be my witnesses that I'm not in with him and I'm not helping him, but that I told you the truth-- that he's a double-dealing liar."

And he finished his speech.

When he'd started, some of the respectable men there wanted to get up and throw the constable out of church so there wouldn't be any

scandal. But my master stopped them and told them all not to bother him under penalty of excommunication. He told them to let him say anything he wanted to. So while the constable was saying all that, my master kept quiet, too.

When he stopped speaking, my master told him if he wanted to say anything more he should go ahead. And the constable said, "I could say plenty more about you and your dirty tricks, but I've said enough for now."

Then the pardoner knelt down in the pulpit, and with his hands folded, and looking up toward heaven, he said: "Lord God, to Whom nothing is hidden and everything is manifest, for Whom nothing is impossible and everything is possible, Thou knowest the truth of how unjustly I have been accused. In so far as I am concerned, I forgive him so that Thou, Oh Lord, may forgive me. Pay no attention to this man who knows not what he says or does. But the harm that has been done to Thee, I beg and beseech Thee in the name of righteousness that Thou wilt not disregard it.

"Because someone here may have been thinking of taking this holy indulgence, and now, believing that the false words of that man are true, they will not take it. And since that would be so harmful to our fellow men, I beg Thee, Lord, do not disregard it; instead, grant us a miracle here. Let it happen in this way: if what that man says is true--that I am full of malice and falseness--let this pulpit collapse with me in it and plunge one hundred feet into the ground, where neither it nor I shall ever be seen again. But if what I say is true--and he, won over by the devil to distrain and deprive those who are here present from such a great blessing--if he is saying false things, let him be punished and let his malice be known to all."

My reverent master had hardly finished his prayer when the crooked constable fell flat on his face, hitting the floor so hard that it made the whole church echo. Then he began to roar and froth at the mouth and to twist it and his whole face, too, kicking and hitting and rolling around all over the floor.

The people's shouts and cries were so loud that no one could hear anyone else. Some were really terrified. Other people were saying, "God help him." And others said, "He got what was coming to him. Anyone who lies like he did deserves it.

Finally, some of the people there (even though I think they were really afraid) went up to him and grabbed hold of his arms, while he was swinging wildly at everyone around him.

Other people grabbed his legs, and they really had to hold him tight because he was kicking harder than a mule. They held him down for quite a while. There were more than fifteen men on top of him, and he was still trying to hit them; and if they weren't careful he would punch them in the nose.

All the time that master of mine was on

his knees up in the pulpit with his hands and eyes fixed on heaven, caught up by the Holy Spirit. And all the noise in the church--the crying and shouting--couldn't bring him out of that mystical trance.

Those good men went up to him, and by shouting they aroused him and begged him to help that poor man who was dying. They told him to forget about the things that had happened before and the other man's awful words because he had been paid back for them. But if he could somehow do something that would take that man out of his misery and suffering, to do it--for God's sake--because it was obvious that the other man was guilty and that the pardoner was innocent and had been telling the truth, since the Lord had shown His punishment right there when he'd asked for revenge.

The pardoner, as if waking from a sweet dream, looked at them and looked at the guilty man and all the people there, and very slowly he said to them: "Good men, you do not need to pray for a man in whom God has given such a clear sign of Himself. But since He commands us not to return evil for evil and to forgive those who harm us, we may confidently ask Him to do what He commands us to do. We may ask His Majesty to forgive this man who offended Him by putting such an obstacle in the way of the holy faith. Let us all pray to Him."

And so he got down from the pulpit and urged them to pray very devoutly to Our Lord, asking Him to forgive that sinner and bring back his health and sanity and to cast the devil out of him if, because of his great sins, His Majesty had permitted one to go in.

They all got down on their knees in front of the altar, and with the clergy there they began to softly chant a litany. My master brought the cross and the holy water, and after he had chanted over him, he held his hands up to heaven and tilted his eyes upward so that the only thing you could see was a little of their whites. Then he began a prayer that was as long as it was pious. And it made all the people cry (just like the sermons at Holy Week, when the preacher and the audience are both fervent). And he prayed to God, saying that it was not the Lord's will to give that sinner death but to bring him back to life and make him repent. And since the man had been led astray by the devil but was now filled with the thought of death and his sins, he prayed to God to forgive him and give him back his life and his health so he could repent and confess his sins.

And when this was finished, he told them to bring over the indulgence, and he put it on the man's head. And right away that sinner of a constable got better, and little by little he began to come to. And when he was completely back in his senses, he threw himself down at the pardoner's feet and asked his forgiveness. He confessed that the devil had commanded him to say what he did and had put the very words in his mouth. First, to hurt him and get revenge. Secondly--and mainly--because the devil himself would really be hurt by all the good that could be done here if the pardons were bought up.

My master forgave him, and they shook hands. And there was such a rush to buy up the pardons that there was hardly a soul in the whole place that didn't get one: husbands and wives, sons and daughters, boys and girls.

The news of what had happened spread around to the neighboring towns, and when we got to them, he didn't have to give a sermon or even go to the church. People came right up to the inn to get them as if they were going out of style. So in the ten or twelve places we went to around there, my master sold a good thousand indulgences in each place without even preaching a sermon.

While the "miracle" was happening, I have to admit that I was astonished, too, and I got taken in just like the others. But when I saw the way my master and the constable laughed and joked about the business later, I realized that it had all been cooked up by my sharp and clever master.

And even though I was only a boy, it really amused me, and I said to myself: I'll bet these shysters do this all the time to innocent people.

Well, to be brief, I stayed with my fifth master about four months, and I had some hard times with him, too.

VI - How Lazaro Went to Work for a Chaplain and What Happened to Him Then

After this I took up with a man who painted tambourines. He wanted me to grind the colors for him, and I had my trials with him, too.

By now I was pretty well grown up. And one day when I went into the cathedral, a chaplain there gave me a job. He put me in charge of a donkey, four jugs, and a whip, and I began to sell water around the city. This was the first step I took up the ladder to success: my dreams were finally coming true. On weekdays I gave my master sixty coppers out of what I earned, while I was able to keep everything I got above that. And on Saturdays I got to keep everything I made.

I did so well at the job that after four years of it, watching my earnings very carefully, I saved enough to buy myself a good secondhand suit of clothes. I bought a jacket made out of old cotton, a frayed coat with braid on the sleeves and an open collar, a cape that had once been velvety, and an old sword--one of the first ones ever made in Cuellar. When I saw how good I looked in my gentleman's clothes, I told my mas-

ter to take back his donkey: I wasn't about to do
that kind of work any more.

VII - How Lazaro Went to Work for a Constable and Then What Happened to Him

After I left the chaplain I was taken on as bailiff by a constable. But I didn't stay with him very long: the job as too dangerous for me. That's what I decided after some escaped criminals chased me and my master with clubs and rocks. My master stood there and faced them, and they beat him up, but they never did catch me. So I quit that job.

And while I was trying to think of what sort of a life I could lead so that I could have a little peace and quiet and save up something for my old age, God lit up my path and put me on the road to success. With the help of some friends and other people, all the trials and troubles I'd gone through up till then were finally compensated for, seeing as how I got what I wanted: a government job. And no one ever gets ahead without a job like that.

And that's what I've been doing right up to now: I work in God's service--and yours, too. What I do is announce the wines that are being sold around the city. Then, too, I call out at auctions and whenever anything lost. And I go along with the people who are suffering for righteousness' sake and call out their crimes: I'm a town crier, to put it plainly.

It's been a good job, and I've done so well at it that almost all of this sort of work comes to me. In fact, it's gotten to the point where if someone in the city has wine or anything else to

put up for sale, they know it won't come to anything unless Lazarillo of Tormes is in on it.

About this time that gentleman, the Archpriest of San Salvador (your friend and servant), began to notice my abilities and how I was making a good living. He knew who I was because I'd been announcing his wines, and he said he wanted me to marry a maid of his. And I saw that only good, profitable things could come from a man like him, so I agreed to go along with it.

So I married her, and I've never regretted it. Because besides the fact that she's a good woman and she's hardworking and helpful, through my lord, the archpriest, I have all the help and favors I need. During the year he always gives her a few good- sized sacks of wheat, meat on the holidays, a couple loaves of bread sometimes, and his socks after he's through with them. He had us rent a little house right next to his, and on Sundays and almost every holiday we eat at his place.

But there have always been scandalmongers, and I guess there always will be, and they won't leave us in peace. They talk about I don't know what all--they say that they've seen my wife go and make up his bed and do his cooking for him. And God bless them, but they're a bunch of liars.

Because, besides the fact that she's the kind of woman who's hardly happy about these gibes, my master made me a promise, and I think he'll keep it. One day he talked to me for a long time in front of her, and he said to me:

"Lazaro of Tormes, anyone who pays attention to what gossips say will never get ahead. I'm telling you this because I wouldn't be at all surprised if someone did see your wife going in and out of my house. In fact, the reason she goes in is very much to your honor and to hers: and that's the truth. So forget what people say. Just think of how it concerns you--I mean, how it benefits you."

"Sir," I said, "I've decided to be on the side of good men. It is true that some of my friends have told me something of that. The truth is, they've sworn for a fact that my wife had three children before she married me, speaking with reverence to your grace since she's here with us."

Then my wife began to scream and carry on so much that I thought the house with us in it was going to fall in. Then she took to crying, and she cursed the man who had married us. It got so bad that I'd rather I'd died than have let those words of mine slip out. But with me on one side and my master on the other, we talked to her and begged her so much that she finally quit her crying. And I swore to her that as long as I lived I'd never mention another word about the business. And I told her I thought it was perfectly all right--in fact, that it made me happy--for her to go in and out of his house both day and night because I was so sure of her virtue. And so we were all three in complete agreement.

So, right up to today we've never said another word about the affair. In fact, when I see that someone wants to even start talking about it, I cut him short, and I tell him: "Look, if you're my friend, don't tell me something that will make me mad because anyone who does that isn't my friend at all. Especially if they're trying to cause trouble between me and my wife. There's nothing and nobody in the world that I love more than her. And because of her, God gives me all sorts of favors--many more than I deserve. So I'll swear to God that she's as good a woman as any here in Toledo, and if anyone tells me otherwise, I'm his enemy until I die."

So no one ever says anything to me, and I keep peace in my house.

That was the same year that our victorious emperor came to this illustrious city of Toledo and held his court here, and there were all sorts of celebrations and festivities, as you must have heard.

Well, at this time I was prosperous and at the height of all good fortune.

VIII - In Which Lazaro Tells of the Friendship He Struck up in Toledo with Some Germans and What Happened to Them

(The following is the first chapter of an anonymous sequel to *Lazarillo of Tormes*, published in 1555. This chapter became attached to the original work in later editions, but is not to be considered part of the first *Lazarillo*. It is presented here because it serves as a bridge between the first *Lazarillo of Tormes* and the second part by Juan de Luna--TRANSLATOR)

At this time I was prosperous and at the height of all good fortune. And because I always carried a good-sized pan full of some of the good fruit that is raised in this land as a sign of what I was announcing, I gathered so many friends and benefactors around me, both natives and foreigners, that wherever I went no door was closed to me. The people were so kind to me that I believe if I had killed a man then, or had found myself in difficult straits, everyone would have come to my side, and those benefactors would have given me every sort of aid and assistance. But I never left them with their mouths dry because I took them to the places where they could find the best of what I spread throughout the city. And there we lived the good life and had fine times together: we would often walk into a place on our own two feet and go out on the feet of other people. And the best part of it was that all this time Lazaro of Tormes didn't spend a damned cent, and his friends wouldn't let him spend anything. If I ever started to open my purse, pretending that I wanted to pay, they were offended, and they would look at me angrily and say, *"Nite, nite, Asticot, lanz."* They were scolding me, saying that when they were there no one would have to pay a cent.

I was, frankly, in love with those people. And not only because of that, but because whenever we got together they were always filling my pockets and my shirt full of ham and legs of mutton-- cooked in those good wines--along with many spices and huge amounts of beef and bread. So in my house my wife and I always had enough for an entire week. With all this, I remembered the past times when I was hungry, and I praised God and gave thanks that things and times like those pass away. But, as the saying goes, all good things must come to an end. And that's how this turned out. Because they moved the great court, as they do now and then, and when they were leaving, those good friends of mine urged me to go with them, and they said they would give me their help. But I remembered the proverb: Better certain evil than

doubtful good. So I thanked my friends for their good wishes, and with a great deal of clapping on the shoulders and sadness, I said goodbye to them. And I know that if I hadn't been married I would never have left their company because they were the salt of the earth and the kind of people that were really to my liking. The life they lead is a pleasant one. They aren't conceited or presumptuous; they have no hesitation or dislike for going into any wine cellar, with their hats off if the wine deserves it. They are simple, honest people, and they always have so much that I hope God gives me no less when I'm really thirsty.

But the love I had for my wife and my land ("The land you are born in, . . ." as they say) held me back. So I stayed in this city, and although I was well known by the people who lived here, I missed the pleasure of my friends and the court. Still, I was happy, and even happier when my family line was extended by the birth of a beautiful little girl that my wife had then. And although I was a little suspicious, she swore to me that the child was mine. But then fortune thought it had forgotten me long enough, and it decided to show me its cruel, angry, harsh face once more and disturb these few years of good, peaceful living by bringing others of affliction and bitterness. Oh, almighty God! Who could write about such a terrible misfortune and such a disastrous fall without letting the inkwell rest and wiping his eyes with the quill?

Second Part of the Life of Lazarillo of Tormes

θ

Juan de Luna

SECOND PART
OF THE LIFE OF
LAZARILLO
OF TORMES

Drawn Out Of The
Old Chronicles
Of Toledo

By J. DE LUNA, Castilian
and Interpreter of the
Spanish Language

Dedicated to the Most Illustrious
Princess
HENRIETTE DE ROHAN

In PARIS

In the House of ROLET BOU-
TONNE,
in the Palace,
in the Gallery of the Prisoners;
Near the Chancery

M. DC. XX.
By Grant of the King

Letter of Dedication
TO THE
MOST ILLUSTRIOUS
PRINCESS
HENRIETTE DE ROHAN
MOST ILLUSTRIOUS AND EXCELLENT
PRINCESS.

It is common among all writers to dedicate their works to someone who may shelter those works with their authority and defend them with their power. Having decided to bring to light the Second Part of the life of the great Lazaro of Tormes, a mirror and standard of Spanish sobriety, I have dedicated and do dedicate it to Your Excellency, whose authority and power may shelter this poor work (poor, since it treats of Lazaro) and to prevent its being torn apart and abused by biting, gossiping tongues which with their infernal wrath attempt to wound and stain the most sincere and simple wills. I confess my boldness in dedicating such a small work to such a great princess; but its sparseness brings its own excuse--which is the necessity for greater and more effective shelter-- and the kindness of Your Excellency, the pardon. So I humbly beseech Your Excellency to take this small service, putting your eyes on the desire of him who offers it, which is and will be to use my life and strength in your service.

Of whom I am a very humble servant,

J. DE LUNA

To The Reader

The reason, dear reader, that the Second Part of Lazarillo of Tormes is going into print is that a little book has come into my hands that touches on his life but has not one word of truth in it. Most of it tells how Lazaro fell into the sea, where he changed into a fish called a tuna. He lived in the sea for many years and married another tuna, and they had children who were fishes like their father and mother. It also tells about the wars of the tuna, in which Lazaro was the captain, and about other foolishness both ridiculous and erroneous, stupid and with no basis in truth. The person who wrote it undoubtedly wanted to relate a foolish dream or a dreamed-up foolishness.

This book, I repeat, was the prime motivation for my bringing to light this Second Part, exactly as I saw it written in some notebooks in the rogues' archives in Toledo, without adding or subtracting anything. And it is in conformity with what I heard my grandmother and my aunts tell, and on which I was weaned, by the fireside on cold winter nights. And as further evidence, they and the other neighbors would often argue over how Lazaro could have stayed

119

under water so long (as my Second Part relates) without drowning. Some said he could have done it, others said he could not: those who said he could cited Lazaro himself, who says the water could not go into him because his stomach was full all the way up to his mouth. One good old man who knew how to swim, and who wanted to prove that it was feasible, interposed his authority and said he had seen a man who went swimming in the Tagus, and who dived and went into some caverns where he stayed from the time the sun went down until it came up again, and he found his way out by the sun's glow; and when all his friends and relatives had grown tired of weeping over him and looking for his body to give him a burial, he came out safe and sound.

The other difficulty they saw about his life was that nobody recognized that Lazaro was a man, and everyone who saw him took him for a fish. A good canon (who, since he was a very old man, spent all day in the sun with the weavers) answered that this was even more possible basing his statement on the opinion of many ancient and modern writers, including Pliny, Phaedo, Aristotle, and Albertus Magnus, who testify that in the sea there are some fish of which the males are called Tritons, and the females Nereids, and they are all called mermen: from the waist up they look exactly like men, and from the waist down they are like fish. And I say that even if this opinion were not held by such well-qualified writers, the license that the fishermen had from the Inquisitors would be a sufficient excuse for the ignorance of the Spanish people, because it would be a matter for the Inquisition if they doubted something that their lordships had consented to be shown as such.

About this point (even though it lies outside of what I am dealing with now) I will tell of something that occurred to a farmer from my region. It happened that an Inquisitor sent for him, to ask for some of his pears, which he had been told were absolutely delicious. The poor country fellow didn't know what his lordship wanted of him, and it weighed so heavily on him that he fell ill until a friend of his told him what was wanted. He jumped out of bed, ran to his garden, pulled up the tree by the roots, and sent it along with the fruit, saying that he didn't want anything at his house that would make his lordship send for him again. People are so afraid of them--and not only laborers and the lower classes, but lords and grandees--that they all tremble more than leaves on trees when a soft, gentle breeze is blowing, when they hear these names: Inquisitor, Inquisition. This is what I have wanted to inform the reader about so that he can answer when such questions are aired in his presence, and also I beg him to think of me as the chronicler and not the author of this work, which he can spend an hour of his time with. If he enjoys it, let him wait for the Third Part about the death and testament of Lazarillo, which is the best of all. And if not, I have nevertheless done my best. *Vale.*

I - Where Lazaro Tells about How He Left Toledo to Go to the War of Algiers

"A prosperous man who acts unwisely should not be angry when misfortune comes." I'm writing this epigram for a reason: I never had the mentality or the ability to keep myself in a good position when fortune had put me there. Change was a fundamental part of my life that remained with me both in good, prosperous times and in bad, disastrous ones. As it was, I was living as good a life as any patriarch ever had, eating more than a friar who has been invited out to dinner, drinking more than a thirsty quack doctor, better dressed than a priest, and in my pocket were two dozen pieces of silver--more reliable than a beggar in Madrid. My house was as well stocked as a beehive filled with honey, my daughter was born with the odor of saintliness about her, and I had a job that even a pew opener in the church at Toledo would have envied.

Then I heard about the fleet making ready to sail for Algiers. The news intrigued me, and like a good son I decided to follow in the footsteps of my good father Tome Gonzalez (may he rest in peace). I wanted to be an example--a model--for posterity. I didn't want to be remembered for leading that crafty blind man, or for nibbling on the bread of the stingy priest, or for serving that penniless squire, or even for calling out other people's crimes. The kind of example I wanted to be was one who would show those blind Moors the error of their ways, tear open and sink those arrogant pirate ships, serve under a valiant captain who belonged to the Order of Saint John (and I did enlist with a man like that as his valet, with the condition that everything I took from the Moors I would be able to keep, and it turned out that way). Finally, what I wanted to do was to be a model for shouting at and rousing the troops with our war cry: "Saint James be with us.... Attack, Spaniards!"

I said good-by to my adoring wife and my dear daughter. My daughter begged me not to forget to bring her back a nice Moorish boy, and my wife told me to be sure to send, by the first messenger, a slave girl to wait on her and some Barbary gold to console her while I was gone. I asked my lord the archpriest's permission, and I put my wife and daughter in his charge so he would take care of them and provide for them. He promised me he would treat them as his very own.

I left Toledo happy, proud, and content, full of high hopes--the way men are when they go to war. With me were a great number of friends and neighbors who were going on the same expedition, hoping to better their fortunes. We arrived at Murcia with the intention of going to Cartagena to embark. And there something happened me that I had no desire for. I saw that fortune had put me at the top of its whimsical wheel and with its usual swiftness had pushed me to the heights of worldly prosperity, and now it was beginning to throw me down to the very bottom.

It happened that when I went to an inn, I saw a half-man who, with all the loose and knotted threads hanging from his clothes, had more the appearance of an old goat than a man. His

hat was pulled down so far you couldn't see his face, his cheek was resting on his hand, and one leg was lying on his sword, which was in a half scabbard made of strips of cloth. He had his hat cocked jauntily over one ear (there was no crown on it, so all the hot air coming out of his head could evaporate). His jacket was cut in the French style--so slashed there wasn't a piece big enough to wrap a mustard seed in. His shirt was skin: you could see it through the lattice work of his clothes. His pants were the same material. As for his stockings, one was green and the other red, and they barely covered his ankles. His shoes were in the barefoot style: worn both up and down. By a feather sewn in his hat, the way soldiers dressed, I suspected that he was, in fact, a soldier.

With this thought in mind, I asked him where he was from and where he was going. He raised his eyes to see who was asking, and we both recognized each other: it was the squire I had served under at Toledo. I was astonished to see him in that suit.

When the squire saw my look of amazement, he said: "I'm not surprised to see how startled you are to see me this way, but you won't be when I tell you what happened to me from that day I left you in Toledo until today. As I was going back to the house with the change from the doubloon to pay my creditors, I came across a veiled woman who pulled at my cloak and, sighing and sobbing, pleaded with me to help her out of the plight she was in. I begged her to tell me her troubles, saying that it would take her longer to tell them than for me to take care of them. Still crying, and with a maidenly blush, she told me that the favor I could do for her (and she prayed that I would do it) was to go with her to Madrid where, according to what people had told her, the man was staying who had not only dishonored her but had taken all her jewelry without fulfilling his promise to mar-

ry her. She said that if I would do this for her, she would do for me what a grateful woman should. I consoled her as best I could, raising her hopes by telling her that if her enemy were to be found anywhere in this world, she would be avenged.

"Well, to make a long story short, we went straight to the capital, and I paid her expenses all the way. The lady knew exactly where she was going, and she led me to a regiment of soldiers who gave her an enthusiastic welcome and took her to the captain, and there she signed up as a 'nurse' for the men. Then she turned to me, and with a brazen look said, 'All right, fathead. Now push off!' When I saw that she had tricked me, I flew into a rage, and I told her that if she were a man instead of a woman I would tear her heart out by the roots. One of the soldiers standing there came up and thumbed his nose at me, but he didn't dare to strike me because if he had they would have had to bury him on the spot.

When I saw how badly that business was turning out, I left without saying another word, but I walked out a little faster than usual to see if any brawny soldier was going to follow me so that I could kill him. Because if I had fought that first little soldier boy and killed him (which I would have done, without any doubt), what honor or glory would there have been in it for me? But if the captain or some bully had come out, I would have sliced more holes in them than there are grains of sand in the sea. When I saw that none of them dared to follow me, I left, very pleased with myself. I looked around for work, and since I couldn't find any good enough for a man of my station, here I am like this. It is true that I could have been a valet or an escort to five or six seamstresses, but I would starve to death before I'd take a job like that."

My good master finished by telling me that, since he hadn't been able to find any merchants from his home town to lend him money, he was penniless, and he didn't know where he was going to spend the night. I caught his hint and offered to let him share my bed and my supper. He called my hand. When we were ready to

go to sleep, I told him to take his clothes off the bed because it was too small for so many varmints. The next morning, wanting to get up without making any noise, I reached for my clothes--in vain. The traitor had taken them and vanished. I lay in bed, thinking I was going to die from pure misery. And it might have been better if I had died because I could have avoided all those times I was in agony later.

I started shouting, "Thief! Thief!" The people in the house came up and found me naked as a jaybird, looking in every corner of the room for something to cover myself with. They all laughed like fools, while I was swearing like a mule driver. I damned to hell that thieving bragger who had kept me up half the night telling about all the splendor of himself and his ancestors. The remedy that I took (since no one was giving me any) was to see if I could use that hot-air merchant's clothes until God furnished me with some others. But they were a labyrinth, with no beginning or end to them. There was no difference between the pants and the jacket. I put my legs in the sleeves and used the pants as a coat, and I didn't forget the stockings: they looked more like a court clerk's sleeves--loose enough to put his bribes in. The shoes were like fetters around my ankles: they didn't have any soles. I pulled the hat down over my head, putting the bottom side up so it wouldn't be so

grimy. I won't say a word about the insects running all over me--either the crawling infantry or
the galloping cavalry.

In this shape I went to see my master,
since he had sent for me. He was astonished to
see the scarecrow that walked in, and he laughed
so hard his rear tether let loose, and--royal flush.
Out of respect for him, I think we should pass
over that in silence. After a thousand unsuccess-
ful attempts to talk, he asked me why I was
wearing a disguise. I told him, and the result
was that instead of pitying me, he swore at me
and threw me out of his house. He said that just
as I had let that man come in and sleep in my
bed, one day I would let someone else in, and
they would rob him.

II - How Lazaro Embarked at Cartagena

By nature I didn't last very long with my masters. And it was that way with this one, too, although I wasn't to blame. So there I was, miserable, all alone, and in despair; and with the clothes I was wearing everyone scoffed and made fun of me. Some people said to me, "That's not a bad little hat you have, with its back door. It looks like an old Dutch lady's bonnet."

Others said, "Your rags are certainly stylish. They look like a pigsty: so many other fat little ones are in there with you that you could kill and salt them and send them home to your wife."

One of the soldiers--a packhandler--said to me, "Mr. Lazarillo, I'll swear to God your stockings really show off your legs. And your sandals look like the kind the barefoot friars wear."

A constable replied, 'That's because this gentleman is going to preach to the Moors."

They kept teasing and taunting me so much that I was nearly ready to go back home. But I didn't because I thought it would be a poor war if I couldn't get more than I would lose. What hurt me most was that everyone avoided me like the plague. We embarked at Cartagena: the ship was large and well stocked. They unfurled the sails, and a wind caught them and sent the ship skimming along at a good clip. The land disappeared from sight, and a cross wind lashed the sea and sent waves hurling up to the clouds. As the storm increased, we began losing hope; the captain and crew gave us up for lost. Everyone was weeping and wailing so much I thought we were at a sermon during Holy Week. With all the clamor no one could hear any of the orders that were given. Some people were running to one place, others to another: it was as noisy and chaotic as a blacksmith's shop. Everyone was saying confession to whoever they could. There was even one man who confessed to a prostitute, and she absolved him so well you would have thought she had been doing it for a hundred years.

Churning water makes good fishing, they say. So when I saw how busy everyone was, I said to myself: If I die, let it be with my belly full. I wandered down to the bottom of the ship, and there I found huge quantities of bread, wine, meat pies, and preserves, with no one paying any attention to them. I began to eat everything and to fill my stomach so it would be stocked up to last me till judgment day. A soldier came up and

asked me to give him confession. He was astonished to see how cheerful I was and what a good
appetite I had, and he asked how I could eat
when death was so near. I told him I was doing
it so that all the sea water I would drink when I
drowned wouldn't make me sick. My simplicity
made him shake with laughter from head to foot.
I confessed a number of people who didn't utter
a word with the agony they were in, and I didn't
listen to them because I was too busy eating.

The officers and people of high rank escaped safely in a skiff, along with two priests
who were on board. But my clothes were so bad

that I couldn't fit inside. When I had my fill of eating, I went over to a cask full of good wine and transferred as much as I could hold into my stomach. I forgot all about the storm, myself, and everything. The ship started to sink and the water came pouring in as though it had found its home. A corporal grabbed my hands and as he was dying he asked me to listen to a sin he wanted to confess. He said he hadn't carried out a penance he had been given, which was to make a pilgrimage to Our Lady of Loreto, even though he had had many opportunities to do it. And now that he wanted to, he couldn't. I told him that with the authority vested in me, I would commute his penance, and that instead of going to Our Lady of Loreto, he could go to Santiago.

"Oh, sir," he said. "I would like to carry out that penance, but the water is starting to come into my mouth, and I can't."

"If that's the way it is," I said, "the penance I give you is to drink all the water in the sea."

But he didn't carry that out either because there were many men there who drank as much as he did. When it came up to my mouth I said to it: Try some other door, this one is not opening. And even if it had opened, the water couldn't have gotten in, because my body was so full of wine it looked like a stuffed pig. As the ship broke apart a huge swarm of fish came in.

It was as though they were being given aid from the bodies on board. They ate the flesh of those miserable people who had been overcome by a drop in the ocean, as if they were grazing in the county pasture. They wanted to try me out, but I drew my trustworthy sword and without stopping to chat with such a low-class mob, I laid into them like a donkey in a new field of rye.

They hissed at me: "We're not trying to hurt you. We only want to see if you taste good."

I worked so hard that in less than half-a-quarter of an hour I killed more than five hundred tuna, and they were the ones that wanted to make a feast out of the flesh of this sinner. The live fish began to feed on the dead ones, and they left Lazaro's company when they saw it wasn't a very profitable place to be. I found myself lord of the sea, with no one to oppose me. I ran around from one place to another, and I saw things that were unbelievable: huge piles of skeletons and bodies. And I found a large number of trunks full of jewels and gold, great heaps of weapons, silks, linens, and spices. I was longing for it all and sighing because it wasn't back at home, safe, so that, as the buffoon says, I could eat my bread dipped in sardines.

I did what I could, but that was nothing. I opened a huge chest and filled it full of coins and precious jewels. I took some ropes from the piles of them there and tied up the chest, and then I knotted other ropes together until I had one I thought was long enough to reach to the surface of the water. If I can get all this treasure out of here, I thought to myself, there won't be a tavernkeeper in the world better off than I'll be. I'll build up my estate, live off my investments, and buy a summer house in Toledo. They'll call my wife "Madam," and me they'll call "Sir." I'll marry my daughter to the richest pastrycook in town. Everyone will come to congratulate me,

and I'll tell them that I worked hard for it, and
that I didn't take it out of the bowels of the earth
but from the heart of the sea. That I didn't get
damp with sweat but drenched as a dried her-
ring. I have never been as happy in my life as I

was then, and I wasn't even thinking about the
fact that if I opened my mouth I would stay
down there with my treasure, buried till hell
froze over.

III - How Lazaro Escaped from the Sea

I saw how near I was to death, and I was horrified; how near I was to being rich, and I was overjoyed. Death frightened me, and the treasure delighted me. I wanted to run away from the first and enjoy the second. I tore off the rags that my master, the squire, had left me for the services I had done him. Then I tied the rope to my foot and began to swim (I didn't know how to do that very well, but necessity put wings on my feet and oars on my hands). The fish there gathered around to nip at me, and their prodding was like spurs that goaded me on. So with them nipping and me galloping, we came up to the surface of the water, where something happened that was the cause of all my troubles. The fish and I were caught up in some nets that some fishermen had thrown out, and when they felt the fish in the nets they pulled so mightily, and water began to flow into me just as mightily, so that I couldn't hold out, and I started to drown. And I would have drowned if the sailors had not pulled the booty on board with their usual speed. What a God-awful taste! I have never drunk anything that bad in my entire life. It tasted like the archpriest's piss my wife made me drink once, telling me it was good Ocaña wine.

With the fish on board and myself as well, the fishermen began to pull on the line and discovered the spool (as the saying goes). They found me tangled up in the rope and were astonished, and they said, "What sort of fish is this? Its face looks like a man's. Is it the devil or a ghost? Let's pull on that rope and see what he has fastened to his foot."

The fishermen pulled so hard that their ship started to sink. When they saw the trouble they were in, they cut the rope, and at the same time they cut off Lazaro's hopes of ever becoming one of the landed gentry. They turned me upside down so I would empty out the water I had drunk and the wine, too. They saw that I wasn't dead (which was by no means the worst that could have happened to me), so they gave me a little wine, and I came back to life like a lamp with kerosene poured in. They asked me all kinds of questions, but I didn't answer a word until they gave me something to eat. When I got my breath back, the first thing I asked them about was the shackles that were tied to my foot. They told me that they had cut them to get out of the danger they had been in. Troy was lost and so were all of Lazaro's great desires: and right then his troubles, cares, and hardships began. There is nothing in the world worse than to have

fancied yourself rich, on top of the world, and then to suddenly find yourself poor and at the bottom of the ladder

I had built my castles on the water, and it had sunk them all. I told the fishermen what both of us lost when they had cut off my shackles. They were so angry that one of them nearly went mad. The shrewdest one said they should throw me back into the sea and wait for me there until I came up again. They all agreed with him, and even though I objected strongly, their minds were made up: they said that since I knew the way, it would be easy for me (as if I would be going to the pastry shop or the tavern!).

They were so blinded by their greed that they would have thrown me out if my fortune (or misfortune) had not arranged for a ship to come up to us to help carry back the fish. They all kept quiet so that the others wouldn't find out about the treasure they had discovered. But they had to leave off their evil plan for the moment. They brought their boats to shore, and they threw me back with the fish to hide me, intending to hunt for me again when they could. Later, two of them picked me up and carried me to a little hut nearby. One man who didn't know the secret asked them what I was. They said I was a monster that had been caught with the tuna. When they had me inside that miserable pigsty, I begged them to give me some rags to cover my naked body so I could be presentable.

You can do that," they said, "after you've settled your account with the hostess."

At the time I didn't understand their gibberish. The fame of the monster spread through the countryside, and many people came to the hut to see me. But the fishermen didn't want to show me; they said they were waiting for permission from the bishops and the Inquisition and that, until then, it was entirely out of the question. I was stupefied. I didn't know what they were planning, and so I didn't know what to say or do. The same thing happened to me that happens to the cuckold: he is the last to find out. Those devils cooked up a scheme that Satan

himself wouldn't have thought of. But that requires a new chapter and a new look.

IV - How They Took Lazaro
through Spain

Opportunity makes the thief. And when the fishermen realized they had such a good opportunity, they grabbed it lock, stock, and barrel. When they saw that so many people were gathering around the new fish, they decided to win back what they had lost when they cut the rope from my foot. So they sent word to the ministers of the Inquisition, asking permission to show a fish with a man's face through all of Spain. And when they offered those gentlemen a present of the best fish they had caught, they were given that permission immediately. Meanwhile, our friend Lazaro was thanking God for having taken him out of the belly of the whale. (And that was a great miracle since my ability and knowledge were not very good, and I swam like a lead brick.)

Four of the fishermen grabbed hold of me, and they seemed more like executioners--the kind that crucified Christ--than men. They tied up my hands, and then they put a mossy wig and beard on me, and they didn't forget the mustache: I looked like a garden statue. They wrapped my feet in seaweed, and I saw that they had dressed me up like a stuffed and trussed trout. Then I began to groan and moan over my troubles, complaining to fate or fortune: Why are you always pursuing me? I have never seen or touched you, but if a man can tell the cause by the effects, I know from my experience with you that there is no siren, basilisk, viper, or lioness with her young more cruel than you are. By flattery and caresses you lift men up to the height of your riches and pleasures and then hurtle them into the abyss of all their misery and calamities, and their depths are as low as your favors were high.

One of those cutthroats heard my soliloquy, and with a rasping voice he said to me, "If you say another word, Mr. Tunafish, we'll salt you along with your friends, or we'll burn you as a monster. The Inquisition," he continued, "has told us to take you through the village and towns in Spain and to show you off to everyone as a wonder and monster of nature."

I swore to them that I was no tuna, monster, or anything out of the ordinary. I said that I was a man just like everyone else, and that if I had come out of the ocean it was because I had fallen into it along with the men who drowned while going to make war on Algiers. But they were deaf men, and even worse, because they didn't want to hear. When I saw that my begging was as useless as the soap they use to wash an ass's head, I became patient and waited for time--which cures everything--to cure my trouble, knowing it all came from suffering through that damned metamorphosis.

They put me in a barrel cut in half, made to look like a brigantine. Then they filled it with water that came up to my lips as I sat in it. I couldn't stand up because they had my feet tied with a rope, and one end of it came out between the mesh of that hairy mess of mine so that if I made so much as a peep, they would make me hop and sink like a frog and drink more water than a person with dropsy. I would keep my mouth closed until I felt whoever was pulling on the rope let it go slack. Then I would stick my head out like a turtle, and I learned by what happened to my own.

They showed me like this to everyone, and so many people came to see me (each one paying twenty coppers) that they made two hundred pieces of silver in one day. The more money they made the more they wanted, and they began to be very concerned about my health so they could prolong it. They held a summit conference and discussed whether or not they should take me out of the water at night: they were afraid that with all the wet and cold it might cut my life short, and they loved mine more than their own (because of all the profit they were getting from mine). They decided to keep me in the water all the time because they thought the force of habit would change my nature. So poor Lazaro was like a string of wet rice or the binding on a raft.

I leave to the dear reader's imagination what I went through in this situation: here I was, a captive in this free land, in chains because of the wickedness of those greedy puppeteers. The worst part about it, and what tormented me most, was that I had to pretend to be mute when I really wasn't. I wasn't even able to open my mouth because the instant I did my guard was so alert that without anyone being able to see him, he would fill me up with water, afraid that I would talk.

My meals were dunked bread that the people who came to see me threw in so they could watch me eat. So for the six months I spent in that cooler I didn't get another damned thing to eat: I was dying of hunger. I drank tub water, and since it wasn't very clean it was all the more nourishing--especially because its coldness gave me attacks of diarrhea that lasted me as long as that watery purgatory did.

V - How They Took Lazaro to the Capital

Those torturers took me from city to town, from town to village, from village to farm, happier than a lark with their earnings. They made fun of poor Lazaro, and they would sing: "Hooray, hooray for the fish. He earns our keep while we loaf."

My "coffin" was placed on a cart, and three men went along with me: the mule driver, the man who pulled on the rope whenever I tried to say anything, and the one who told all about me. This last one would make a speech about the strange way they caught me, telling more lies than a tailor at Eastertime. When we were traveling and no one else was around, they let me talk, and that was the only courtesy they showed me. I asked them who the devil had put it in their heads to take me around like that, in a fish bowl. They answered that if they didn't do it I would die on the spot because, since I was a fish, I couldn't live out of water. When I saw how their minds were set on the idea, I decided to be a fish, and I finally convinced myself that I was one: after all, everyone else thought that's what I was, and that the seawater had changed me into one, and they say that the voice of the people is the voice of God. So from then on I was as silent as a man at mass. They took me to the capital, and there they really made a lot of money. Because the people there, being idlers, liked

novelties.

Among all the people who came to see me there were two students. They studied the features of my face very carefully, and then, in a low tone, they said that they would swear on the Bible I was a man and not a fish. And they said if they were the authorities they would get at the naked truth by taking a leather strap to our naked shoulders. I was praying to God with all my heart and soul that they would do it, as long as they could get me out of there. I tried to help them by shouting, 'You scholars are right." But I hardly had my mouth open when my guard pulled me under the water. Everyone's shouting when I ducked (or, rather, when they dunked me) stopped those good scholars from going on with their talk.

They threw bread to me, and I would bolt it down almost before it had a chance to get wet. They didn't give me half of what I could eat. I remembered the feasts I had in Toledo, how well I ate with my German friends, and that good wine I used to announce in the streets. I prayed to God to repeat the miracle of Cana of Galilee and not let me die at the hands of water--my worst enemy. I thought about what those students had said, which no one heard because of the noise. I realized that I was a man, and I never thought otherwise from then on, although my wife had told me many times that I was a beast, and the boys at Toledo used to say, "Mr. Lazaro, pull your hat down a little--we can see your horns."

All this, along with the sauce I was in, had made me doubt whether or not I really was a

man. But after I heard those blessed earthly di-
viners, I had no more doubts about it, and I tried
to escape from the hands of those Chaldeans.

Once, in the dead of night, I saw that my
guards were fast asleep, and I tried to get loose.
But the ropes around me were wet, and I could-
n't. I thought about shouting, but I decided that
that wouldn't work, since the first one who heard
me would seal my mouth with a half-gallon of
water. When I saw that way out cut off, I began
to twist around impatiently in the slough, and I
struggled and pushed so much that the cask

turned over, and me along with it. All the water spilled out, and when I found myself freed I shouted for help.

The fishermen were terrified when they realized what I'd done, and they quickly hit on a solution: they stopped up my mouth by stuffing it full of seaweed. And to muddle my shouts, they began to shout themselves, even louder, calling out, "Help, help, call the law!" And as they were doing all this, they filled the cask back up with water from a nearby well, with unbeliev-able speed. The innkeeper came running out

with a battle-ax, and everyone else at the inn
came out armed with iron pokers and sticks. All
the neighbors came in, along with a constable
and six deputies who happened to be passing by.
The innkeeper asked the sailors what had happened, and they answered that thieves had tried
to steal their fish. And like a madman he began
shouting, "Get the thieves, get the thieves!"
Some went to see if they had gotten out the door;
others went to find out if they were escaping
across the rooftops. And as for me, my custodi-
ans had put me back in my vat.

It happened that the water that spilled
out all ran through a hole in the floor, onto the
bed of a room downstairs where the daughter of
the house was sleeping. Now this girl had been
so moved to charity that she had brought a
young priest in with her to spend the night in
contemplation. They became so frightened
when the deluge fell on the bed and all the people began shouting that they crawled out
through a window as naked as Adam and Eve,
without even a fig leaf to cover their private
parts. There was a full moon, and its brightness
was so great that it could have competed with
the sun. When the people saw them they shouted, "Get the thieves, catch the thieves!" The
deputies and the constable ran after the girl and
the priest and quickly caught up with them because they were barefoot and the stones on the

ground made it difficult for them to run. And in one swoop they led them off to jail. Early next morning the fishermen left Madrid to go to Toledo, and they never did find out what God had done with that simple little maiden and the devout priest.

VI - How They Took Lazaro to Toledo

Man's efforts are vain, his knowledge is nil, and he has no ability when God does not strengthen, teach, and guide him. All my efforts only served to make my guards more wary and careful. The outburst of the night before made them very angry, and they beat me so much along the road that they nearly left me for dead. They said, You damned fish--you were trying to get away. If we weren't so kindhearted, we would kill you. You're like an oak tree that won't give up its acorns unless it's beaten."

The fishermen took me into Toledo, pounded, cursed, and dying of hunger. They found a place to stay, near the square of Zocodover, at the house of a lady whose wines I used to announce. They put me in a room downstairs, and many people came to see me. One of them was my Elvira, leading my daughter by the hand. When I saw them I couldn't hold back two Nile Rivers of tears that flowed from my eyes. I sighed and wept--but to myself so the fishermen wouldn't deprive me of what I loved so much and what I wanted to feast my eyes on. Although it might have been better if those men who took away my voice had taken away my sight, too, because when I looked at my wife carefully I saw--I don't know if I should say it-- she looked like she was about to go into labor. I sat there absolutely amazed, although I shouldn't have been if I had thought about it because my lord the archdeacon told me when I left that city to go to war that he would treat her as if she were his very own. What really bothered me was that I couldn't convince myself that she was pregnant by me because I had been gone for more than a year.

When we were living together she used to say to me, "Lazaro, don't think I'm cheating on you, because if you do you're very wrong." And I was so satisfied that I avoided thinking anything bad about her the way the devil avoids holy water. I spent my life happy and content and not at all jealous (which is a madman's sickness). Time and again I have thought to myself that this business of children is all a matter of belief. Because how many men are there who love children they think are their own when the only thing they have in common is their name? And there are others who hate their children because they get the notion that their wives have put horns on their heads.

I began to count the days and months, and I found the road to my consolation closed off. Then I began to think that my wife might have dropsy. I didn't go on with this pious meditation very long because as soon as she left, two old women began to talk to each other: "What do you think of that archpriestess? She certainly doesn't need her husband around." "Who is the father?" asked the other. 'Who?" answered the first, 'Why, the archpriest. And he's such a good man that, to avoid the scandal that would spread if she gave birth in his house without a husband, he's going to marry her to that foreigner, Pierre, next Sunday, and that fellow will be just as understanding as my friend, Lazaro."

This was the last straw--the *non plus ultra*--of my understanding. My heart began to break out in a sweat in the water, and without being able to lift a hand I fainted in that hogsty.

The water began to pour into me through every door and window, without any resistance. I looked like I was dead (although it was completely against my will, because I wanted to live as long as I could and as long as God would let me, in spite of those damned fishermen and my bad luck).

The fishermen were very upset, and they made every one leave. Then they very quickly lifted my head out of the water. When they saw that I had no pulse and that I'd stopped breathing, they did, too. They started to moan over what they had lost (which was no small amount for them), and they took me out of the cask. Then they tried to make me vomit up all I had drunk, but that was useless because death had come in and closed the door behind. When they saw all their dreams gone up in smoke, they turned as ashen as lilies on the Sunday after Easter. They couldn't think of any way to abet or abate their trials and troubles. The Council of Three finally decreed that the following night they would take me to the river and throw me in with a stone tied around my neck so that what had caused my death would also be my grave.

VII - What Happened to Lazaro on the Way to the Tagus River

Never lose hope no matter how miserable you are, because when you least expect it God will open the doors and windows of His mercy and will show that nothing is impossible for Him, and that He has the knowledge, the ability, and the desire to change the plans of the wicked into healthful, beneficial remedies for those who trust in Him. Those brutal executioners decided that Death wasn't joking (it seldom does), so they put me in a sack, threw me across the back of a donkey like a wineskin--or rather a water-skin, since I was full of water up to my mouth--and started out along the road of Cuesta de Carmen. And they were more sorrowful than if they were going to bury the father who gave them life and the mother who bore them.

It was my good fortune that when they put me on the mule, I was belly side down. Since my head was hanging downward, I began to spew out water as if they had lifted the flood-gates on a dam, or as if I were a drop hammer. I came to, and when I caught my breath I realized that I was out of the water and out of that blast-ed hairy mess. I didn't know where I was or where they were taking me. I only heard them saying, "For our own safety we'll have to find a very deep well so they won't discover him so soon." Then I saw the handwriting on the wall and guessed what was happening. I knew that their bark could be no worse than their bite, and when I heard people approaching I called, "Help, help, for God's sake!"

The people I had noticed were the night

watch, and they ran up when they heard my cries, their swords out and ready. They searched the sack, and they found poor Lazaro--a drenched haddock. Body and soul, they took us all off to jail on the spot: the fishermen were crying to see themselves imprisoned, and I was

laughing to find myself free.

They put them in a cell and me in a bed. The next morning they took our statements. The fishermen confessed that they had carried me all over Spain, but they said that they had done it thinking I was a fish and that they had asked for the Inquisition's permission to do it. I told them the truth of the matter: how those fiends had tied me up so that I couldn't make a peep. They had the archpriest and my good Bridget come to testify as to whether or not I really was the Lazaro of Tormes I said I was. My wife came in first, and she looked me over very carefully, and then said it was true that I did look something like her good husband, but she didn't think I was him because even though I had been an animal, I was more like a drone than a fish, and more like a bullock than a tuna. After saying this she made a deep bow and left.

The attorney for those hangmen said I should be burned because I was undoubtedly a monster, and he was going to prove it.

I thought to myself: What if there really is an enchanter following me and changing me into anything he likes?

The judges told him to be quiet. Then the archpriest came in. He saw me looking as pale and wrinkled as an old lady's belly, and he said he didn't recognize my face or my figure. I refreshed his memory about some past things (many of them secret) that had happened between us; I especially told him to think back on the night he came to my bed naked and said that he was afraid of a ghost in his bedroom, and then crawled into bed between my wife and me. So that I wouldn't go on with these reminders, he confessed that I really was his good friend and servant, Lazaro.

The trial ended with the testimony of the captain who had taken me with him from Toledo. He was one of those who escaped the storm

in a skiff, and he confessed that I was, in fact, his servant Lazaro. The time and place the fishermen said they had fished me out supported that. The judges sentenced them to two hundred whippings apiece and the confiscation of their belongings: a third of it would be given to the King, a third to the prisoners, and a third to Lazaro. They found them with two thousand pieces of silver, two mules, and a cart, and after the costs and expenditures were paid I got two hundred pieces of silver. The sailors were plucked and skinned, and I was rich and happy because I had never in my life been the owner of so much money at one time.

I went to the house of a friend of mine, and after I had downed a few pitchers of wine to get rid of the bad taste of the water and was feeling mellow, I began to strut around like a count and to eat like a king; I was esteemed by my friends, feared by my enemies, and wooed by everyone. My past troubles seemed like a dream to me, my present luck was like a port of leisure, and my future hopes a paradise of delights. Hardships humiliate, prosperity makes a man haughty. For the time those two hundred silver pieces lasted, if the King had called me his cousin I would have taken it as an insult.

When we Spaniards get a silver coin, we're princes, and even if we don't have one we still have the vanity that goes with it. If you ask some shabby beggar who he is, he'll tell you at the very least that he is of noble blood and that his bad luck has him backed into a corner, and that's how this mad world is: it raises those who are on the bottom and lowers those who are on top. But even though it is that way, he won't give in to anyone, he puts only the highest value on himself, and he will die of hunger before he'll work. And if Spaniards do take a job or learn something, they have such contempt for it that either they won't work or, if they do, their work is so bad that you can hardly find a good craftsman anywhere in Spain.

I remember there was a cobbler in Sala-

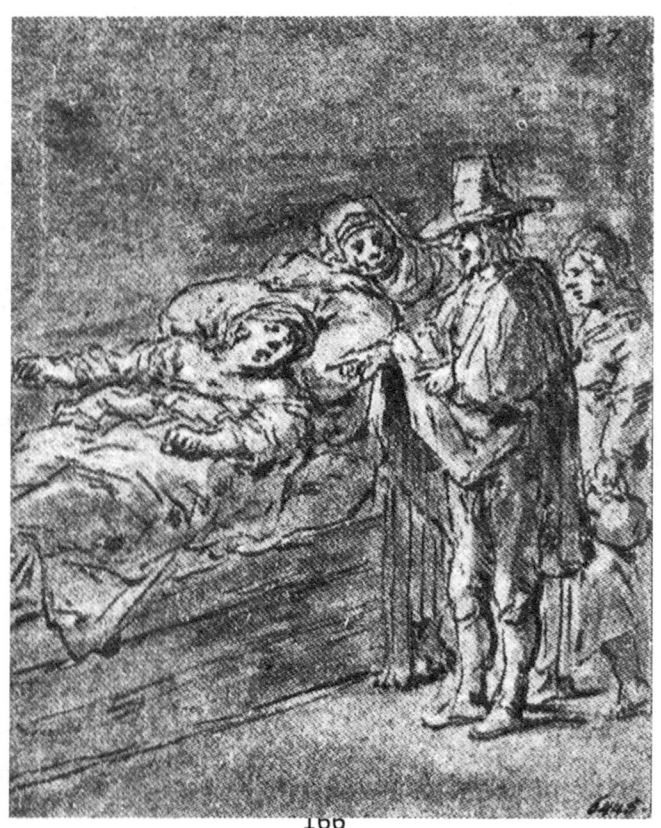

manca, and whenever anyone brought him something to fix, he would deliver a soliloquy, complaining that fate had put him in such straits that he had to work in this lowly position when the good name of his family was so well known all over Spain. One day I asked one of his neighbors who that bragger's parents were. They told me his father was a grape stomper, and in winter a hogkiller, and that his mother was a belly washer (I mean the maid for a tripe merchant).

I bought a worn-out velvet suit and a ragged cast-off cape from Segovia. The sword I wore was so enormous that its tip would unpave the streets as I walked. I didn't want to go and see my wife when I got out of jail so that she would want to see me even more, and also to take revenge for the disdain for me that she was carrying around inside herself. I really thought that when she saw me so well-dressed she would repent and greet me with open arms. But obstinate she was, and obstinate she remained. I found her with a new baby and a new husband. When she saw me she shouted, "Get that damn drenched fish--that plucked goose--out of my sight because, if you don't, I swear on my father's grave that I'll get up and poke his eyes out!"

And I answered very coolly, "Not so fast, Mrs. Streetwalker. If you won't admit I'm your husband, then you're not my wife either. Give me my daughter, and we'll still be friends. I have enough of a fortune now," I went on, "to marry her to a very honorable man."

I thought those two hundred pieces of silver would turn out to be like the fifty silver coins of little Blessed John who, every time he spent them, would find fifty more in his purse. But since I was little Bedeviled Lazaro, it didn't turn out that way with me, as you will see in the next chapter.

The archpriest contested my demand. He said she wasn't mine, and to prove it he showed me the baptismal book, and when it was compared to the marriage records, it was evident that the child had been born four months after I knew my wife. Up to then I had felt as spirited as a stallion, but I suddenly realized they had made an ass of me: my daughter wasn't mine at all. I shook the dust off my feet and washed my hands to show my innocence and that I was leaving for good. I turned my back on them, feeling as content as if I had never known them. I went looking for my friends and told them what had happened; they consoled me--which wasn't hard for them to do.

I didn't want to go back to my job as a town crier because my new velvet clothes had changed my self-esteem. While I was taking a walk to the Visagra gate I met an old woman, a friend of mine, at the gate of the convent of San

Juan de los Reyes. After she greeted me she told me that my wife had softened when she'd found out about all the money I had, especially now that that Frenchman had chastened her.

I begged her to tell me what had happened. She said the archpriest and my wife had talked one day about whether it would be a good idea to take me back in and throw Frenchy out; and they discussed the pros and cons of it. But their discussion was not so secret that the bridegroom didn't hear it. He pretended he hadn't heard a thing, and the next morning he went to work at the olive grove. At noon, when his wife and mine brought his lunch out to him, he pulled off all her clothes, tied her to the trunk of a tree, and gave her more than a hundred lashes. And still not satisfied, he made all her clothes into a bundle, took off her jewelry, and walked away with it all, leaving her tied up, naked and bleeding. She would undoubtedly have died there if the archpriest hadn't sent someone looking for her.

The lady also told me she was absolutely sure that if I arranged for somebody to ask her, she would welcome me back, because she had heard my Elvira say, "Poor me, why didn't I take back my good Lazaro? He was as good as could be. He was never critical or particular, and I could do whatever I wanted."

This was the touch that turned me, and I was thinking of taking the good old woman's advice, but first I wanted to talk it over with my friends.

VIII - How Lazaro Brought a Lawsuit against His Wife

We men are like barnyard hens: if we want to do something good we shout it out and cackle about it; but if it's something bad, we don't want anybody to find out so they won't stop us from doing what we shouldn't. I went to see one of my friends, and I found three of them there together; because after I had come into money, they multiplied like flies. I told them what I wanted to do--go back to my wife and get away from wagging tongues because "Better certain evil than doubtful good." They painted a black picture to me and said I was spineless and that I didn't have a brain in my body because the woman I wanted to live with was a whore, a hussy, a trollop, a slut, and, finally, a devil's mule. (That's what they call a priest's mistress in Toledo.)

My friends said so many things to me and gave me so many arguments that I decided not to beg or even ask my wife. When my good friends (damned friends, anyway) saw that their arguments and advice had done their work, they went even further. They said they were advising me, because I was such a good friend, to remove the spots and the stains on my honor and to defend it, since it had fallen into such bad times, by suing the archpriest and my wife. They said it wouldn't cost so much as a penny since they were lawyers.

One of them was an attorney for lost causes, and he offered me a thousand pieces of silver from the profits. The other one was more knowledgeable because he was a prostitutes' lawyer, and he told me that if he were in my shoes he wouldn't take less than two thousand. The third one assured me (and since he was a bumbailiff, he knew what he was talking about) that he had seen other lawsuits that were less clear, that had brought the people who began them an enormous amount of money. Furthermore, he thought that at the first confrontation that Domine Baccalaureus would fill my hands and anoint the lawyers' to make us withdraw the lawsuit, and that he would beg me to go back to my wife. So I would get more honor and profit from it than if I went back to her on my own.

My friends commended this business to me highly, luring me on with high hopes. I was taken in right then. I didn't know what to say to their sophist arguments, although it really seemed to me that it would be better to forgive and forget than to go to extremes, and that I should carry out the most difficult of God's commandments (the fourth one), which is to love your enemies-- especially since my wife had never acted like an enemy to me. In fact, it was because of her that I had begun to rise in the world and become known by many people who would point at me and say, "There goes that nice fellow, Lazaro."

Because of my wife I was somebody. If the daughter that the archdeacon said wasn't mine, was or wasn't, only God, who looks into men's hearts, knows. It could be that he was fooled just the way I was. And it could happen that some of the people who are reading and laughing over my simpleness so hard they slobber on their beards might be raising the children of some ignorant priest. They might be working, sweating, and striving to leave the very ones rich who will impoverish their honor, and all the time they are so sure that if there is any woman in the world who is faithful, it's their wife. And even your name, dear reader-- Lord Whitehall--might really come from Wittol.

But I don't want to destroy anyone's illusions. All these reflections still weren't enough, so I took out a lawsuit against the archpriest and my wife. Since there was ready money, they had them in jail inside of twenty-four hours: him in the archbishop's prison and her in the public one. The lawyers told me not to worry about the money that that business could cost me since it would all come out of that priest's hide. So, to make it even worse for the priest and to raise the costs, I gave whatever they asked me. They were walking around diligent, solicitous, and energetic. When they smelled my cash, they were like flies on honey: they didn't take a step in vain.

In less than a week the lawsuit had moved far ahead, and my pocketbook had lost as much ground. The evidence was gathered easily because the constables who arrested my wife and the archpriest caught them in the act and had taken them off to jail in their nightshirts, the way they found them. There were many witnesses who told the truth. My good lawyers and counselors and the court clerk saw how thin and weak my pocketbook was getting, and they began to falter. It reached the point where I had to spur them harder than a hired mule to get them to make a move.

The slowdown was so great that when the archpriest and his group heard about it, they started crowing and anointing the hands and feet of my representatives. They seemed like the weights on a clock that were going up just as fast as mine were coming down. They managed it so well that in two weeks the archpriest and my wife were out of jail on bond, and in less than one week more they condemned Lazaro with false witnesses so that he had to apologize, pay the court costs, and be banished from Toledo forever.

I apologized the way I should have, since with only two hundred silver pieces I had taken a lawsuit out against a man who had that much money to burn. I gave them the shirt off my back to help pay the court costs, and I left the city in the raw.

There I was, rich for an instant, suing a dignitary of the Holy Church of Toledo, an undertaking fit only for a prince. I had been respected by my friends, feared by my enemies, in the position of a gentleman who wouldn't put up with a whisper of aspersion. And just as suddenly I found myself thrown out--not from any earthly paradise with figleaves to cover my private parts, but from the place I loved most and where I had gotten so much comfort and pleasure, using some rags I found in a rubbish heap to cover my nakedness.

I took refuge in the common consolation of all unfortunates. I thought that since I was at the bottom of the wheel of fortune I would be certain to go back up. I recall now what I once heard my master, the blind man (who was like a fox whenever he started to preach), say: Every man in the world rose and fell on the wheel of fortune; some followed the movement of the wheel, and others went against it. And there was this difference between them: those who followed the wheel's movement fell as quickly as they rose; and those who went against it, once they reached the top--even if they had to work hard at it--they stayed there longer than the others. According to this, I was going right with the grain--and so quickly that I was barely on top when I found myself in the abyss of misery.

I found myself a picaro--and a real one, since I had only been pretending up to then. And I could really say: Naked was I born, naked am I now, nothing lost and nothing gained.

I started off toward Madrid, begging along the way since that was something I knew how to do very well. So there I was again, back at my trade. I told everyone about my troubles: some felt sorry, others laughed, and some gave me alms. Since I had no wife or children to support, with what they gave me I had more than enough to eat, and to drink, too. That year people had harvested so many grapes for wine that at nearly every door I went to they asked if I wanted anything to drink, because they didn't have any bread to give me. I never refused, and so sometimes I would down a good two gallons of wine before eating anything, and I'd be happier than a girl on the eve of a party.

Let me tell you what I really think: the picaresque life is the only life. There is nothing in the world like it. If rich men tried it, they would give up their estates for it, just the way the ancient philosophers gave up all they possessed to go over to that life. I say "go over" because the life of a philosopher and the life of a picaro is the same. The only difference is that philosophers gave up all they had for their love of that kind of life, and picaros find it without giving up anything. Philosophers abandoned their estates to contemplate natural and divine things, the movements of the heavens, with less distraction; picaros do it to sow all their wild oats. Philosophers threw their goods into the sea; picaros throw them in their stomachs. Philosophers despised those things as vain and transitory; while picaros don't care for them because they bring along cares and work--something that goes against their profession. So the picaresque life is more leisurely than the life of kings, emperors, and popes. I decided to travel this road because it was freer, less dangerous, and never sad.

IX - How Lazaro Became a Baggage Carrier

There is no position, no science or art a man does not have to apply all his intelligence to if he wants to perfect his knowledge of it. Suppose a cobbler has been working at his job for thirty years. Tell him to make you a pair of shoes that are wide at the toe, high at the instep, with laces.

Will he make them? Before you get a pair the way you asked him, your feet will be shriveled. Ask a philosopher why a fly's stool comes out black when it's on a white object and white when it's on something black. He'll turn as red as a maiden who is caught doing it by candle-light, and he won't know what to answer. Or if he does answer this question, he won't be able to answer a hundred other tomfooleries.

Near the town of Illescas, I ran into a fellow who I knew was an archpicaro by the way he looked. I went up to him the way I would to an oracle to ask him how I should act in this new life of mine so I wouldn't be arrested. He said that if I wanted to keep free of the law I should combine Mary's idleness with Martha's work. In other words, if I was going to be a picaro I

179

should also be a kitchenhelper, a brothel servant, a slaughterhouse boy, or a baggage carrier, which was a way of covering up for the picaresque life. Furthermore, he said that because he hadn't done this, even after the twenty years he'd been following his profession, they had just yesterday whipped him up one side and down the other for being a tramp.

I thanked him for the warning and took his advice. When I got to Madrid I bought a porter's strap and stood in the middle of the square, happier than a cat with gibblets. As luck would have it, the first person to put me to work was a maiden (God forgive my lie) about eighteen years old, but more primped up than a novice in a convent. She told me to follow her. She took me down so many streets that I thought she was getting paid for walking or was playing a trick on me. After a while we came to a house that I recognized as one of ill repute when I saw the side door, the patio, and the beastly old maids dancing there.

We went into her cell, and she asked me if I wanted her to pay me for my work before we left. I told her I would wait until we got to the place where I was taking the bundle. I loaded it on my back and started down the road to the Guadalajara gate. She told me to put it in a carriage to go to the Nagera fair. The load was light since it was mainly made up of mortars, cosmetics, and perfume bottles. On the way I found out that she had been in that profession for eight years.

"The first one to prick me," she said, "was

the Father Rector at Seville, where I'm from, and he did it with such devotion that from that day to this I'm very devoted to them. He put me in the charge of a holy woman, and she provided me with everything I needed for more than six months. Then a captain took me from there. And since that time I've been led from pillar to post until here I am, like this. I wish to God I had never left that good father who treated me like a daughter and loved me like his sister. Anyway, I've had to work just to be able to eat."

At this time we came up to a carriage that was about to leave. I put the things I was carrying in it and asked her to pay me for my work. The chatterbox said she would be glad to, and she hauled off and hit me so hard she knocked me to the ground. Then she said, "Are you so stupid that you ask someone of my profession for money? Didn't I tell you before we left the brothel that I would give you satisfaction there for your work if you wanted?"

She jumped into the carriage like a nag and spurred the horses away, leaving me feeling the sting. So there I sat, like a jackass, not sure what had happened to me. I thought that if that job finished as well as it was starting out, I would be rich by the end of the year.

I hadn't even left there when another carriage arrived from Alcala de Henares. The people inside jumped down: they were all whores, students, and friars. One of them belonged to the Franciscan order, and he asked me if I would like to carry his bundle to his monastery. I told him I would be glad to because I saw that he certainly wouldn't trick me the way the whore had done. I loaded it onto my back, and it was so heavy I could barely carry it, but I thought of the payment I would get, and that gave me strength. When we reached the monastery I was very tired because it had been so far. The friar took his bundle and said, "May heaven reward you," and then he closed the door behind him.

I waited for him to come back out and pay me, but when I saw how long he was taking, I knocked on the door. The gatekeeper came out and asked me what I wanted. I told him I wanted to be paid for carrying the bundle I'd brought. He told me to go away, that they didn't pay anything there. As he closed the door he told me not to knock again because it was the hour for meditations, and if I did he would whip me thoroughly. I stood there, stupefied. A poor man-- one of those who were standing inside the vestibule--said to me, "Brother, you might as well go away. These fathers never have any money. They live on what other people give them."

"They can live on whatever they want to, but they'll pay me or I'm not Lazaro of Tormes."

I began to knock again very angrily. The lay brother came out even angrier, and without saying so much as, how do you do? he knocked me to the ground like a ripe pear, and holding me down, he kicked me a good half-dozen times, then pounded me just as much, and left me flattened out as if the clocktower of Saragossa had fallen on top of me.

I lay there, stretched out, for more than a half-hour without being able to get up. I thought about my bad luck and that the strength of that irregular clergyman had been used so badly. He would have been better off serving under His Highness, the King, than living from alms for the poor--although they aren't even good for that since they're so lazy. The Emperor, Charles V, pointed this out when the General of the Franciscans offered him twenty-two-thousand friars, who wouldn't be over forty or under twenty-two years old, to fight in the war. The invincible Emperor answered that he didn't want them because he would have needed twenty-two-thousand pots stew every day to keep them alive, implying that they were more fit for eating than working.

God forgive me, but from that day to this I've hated those clergymen so much that whenever I see them they look to me like lazy drones or sieves that lift the meat out of the stew and leave the broth. I wanted to leave that work, but first I waited there that night, stretched out like a corpse waiting for his funeral.

X - What Happened to Lazaro with an Old Bawd

Feeling faint and dying from hunger, I went up the street very slowly, and as I passed by the Plaza of Cebada I ran into an old devout woman with fangs longer than a wild boar. She came up to me and asked if I wanted to carry a trunk to the house of a friend of hers, saying that it wasn't far away and that she would give me forty coppers. When I heard that, I praised God to hear such sweet words coming from such a foul-smelling mouth as hers: she would give me forty coppers! I told her I would, with pleasure-- but my real pleasure was being able to grab onto those forty coppers rather than to carry anything, since I was more in a condition to be carried than to carry. I loaded the trunk on my back, but it was so big and heavy I could barely lift it. The good old woman told me to handle it carefully because inside were some perfume bottles that she prized highly. I told her not to worry because I would walk very slowly. (And even if I had wanted to I couldn't have done anything else: I was so hungry I could barely waddle.)

We reached the house we were taking the chest to. They were very happy to get it, especially a young maiden, plump and dimpled (I was wishing that after I'd eaten a good meal and was in bed, the lice there looked like her): she smiled happily and said she wanted the trunk in her dressing room. I took it there: the old lady gave her the key and told her to keep it until she got back from Segovia. She said she was going there to visit a relative of hers, and she thought she would be back in four days. She gave the girl a hug before she left and whispered a few words in her ear that turned the maiden as red as a rose. And although I thought that was nice, I would have thought it was nicer if I had had plenty to eat. She said good-by to everyone in the house, and asked the girl's father and mother to forgive her for being so bold. They told her she was welcome there anytime. She gave me forty coppers and whispered in my ear to come back to her house the next morning and I would earn forty more.

I went away, happier than a bride in June. I spent thirty coppers on supper, and kept ten to pay for a room. I thought about the power of money. As soon as that old woman gave me the forty coppers I found myself lighter than the wind, more valiant than Roland, and stronger than Hercules. Oh, money, it is not without reason that most men consider you their God. You are the cause of all good, and the root of all evil. You are the inventor of the arts and the one who keeps them excellent. Because of you some maidens remain pure and other maidens give up their purity. Finally, there is no difficulty in the world difficult for you, no hidden place that you do not penetrate, no mountain you do not level, no humble hill you do not raise up.

The next morning I went to the old lady's house the way she asked me. She told me to go back with her and pick up the trunk she had left the day before. She told the people at the house that she had come back for it because when she

was about a mile from Madrid, on the way to Segovia, she had met her relative who had had the
same idea she did and was coming to visit her,
and that she had to have it now because there
were clean linens in it that she needed for her
relative's room. The plumpish girl gave her back
the key, kissing and hugging her more eagerly

than the first time; and after she had whispered
to her again, they helped me load the trunk on
my back, and it seemed to me lighter than the
day before because my belly was fuller.

As I went down the stairs I stumbled over
something that the Devil must have put there. I
tripped and fell with the baggage, and as I rolled

down to the bottom of the stairs where the parents of the innocent girl were waiting, I broke both my nose and my ribs. With the knocks that damned chest got, it opened up, and inside there appeared a dashing young man with sword and dagger at his side. He was dressed in traveling clothes, without a cloak. His trousers and jacket were of green satin, and in his hat he wore a feather of the same color. He had on red garters with pearl-white stockings and white sandals. He stood up very elegantly, and making a deep bow he walked right out the door. Everyone stood there agape at the sudden vision, and they looked at each other like wooden puppets.

When they came out of their trance, they quickly called two of their sons and told them what had happened. With a great outcry the sons grabbed their swords, and shouted, "Kill him, kill him!" They ran out looking for that dandy, but since he had left in a hurry, they weren't able to catch up with him.

The parents had stayed behind in the house, and they closed the door and went to take revenge on the bawd. But she had heard the noise and knew what the cause of it was, and she went out a back door with the eternal bride-to-be right behind her. So the parents found themselves totally taken in. They came back down to take their revenge out on me, and I was all crippled up, unable to move. If it hadn't been for that, I would have been right behind that fellow who had caused all my damage. The brothers came in sweating and panting, vowing and swearing that since they hadn't caught that wretch, they would kill their sister and the go-between. But when they were told they had gotten away by the back door, there was swearing and cursing everywhere.

One of them said, "If only the Devil himself were here right now with all his hellish throng: I would polish them off like flies. Come on, you devils, come on! But what am I calling you for? I know that where you are, you're so afraid of my temper you wouldn't dare show yourselves here. If I'd seen that coward, I would only have had to breathe hard on him, and he would have blown so far away you'd never hear of him again."

The other one said, "If I had caught up with him, I wouldn't have left a piece of him bigger than his ear. But if he's to be found anywhere in this world--or even if he's not--he won't escape my hands. I'll get him even if he hides in the center of the earth."

They kept on with these boasts and other empty threats, and poor Lazaro was expecting all those heavy clouds to unload on him. But he was more afraid of the ten or twelve little boys there than of those braggers. Everyone, old and young, attacked me in a fury: some kicked me, others hit me with their fists; some pulled my hair, others boxed my ears. My fear hadn't been in vain because the girls stuck long penny needles into me, and that made me cry out at the top of my lungs. The family slaves pinched me until I saw stars.

Some of them said, "Let's kill him."

Others said, "Better yet, let's throw him in the privy."

The clamor was so great it sounded like

they were pulverizing chaff, or that they were hammers in a fulling mill that weren't letting up. When they saw that I was out of breath, they stopped beating me, but they didn't stop threatening me. Since the father was more mature, or more rotten, he told them to leave me alone, and he said that if I would tell the truth about who had robbed him of his honor, they wouldn't hurt me any more. I couldn't do what he asked because I didn't know who the fellow was: I had never even seen him before he'd come out of the casket. Since I didn't say anything, they started in again. And there I was groaning, crying over my bad luck, sighing, and cursing my misfortune since it was always finding new ways to persecute me. I was finally able to tell them to stop and I would tell them the facts of the matter. They did, and I told them to the letter what had happened, but they wouldn't believe the truth.

Seeing that the storm wasn't letting up, I decided to outwit them if I could, and so I promised to show them the villain. They stopped hammering on me and offered me wonders. They asked me what his name was and where he lived. I told them I didn't know his name, much less that of the street he lived on, but if they wanted to carry me (it was impossible for me to go on foot because of the way they had beaten me), I would show them his house. They were delighted, and they gave me a little wine, so that

I recovered my spirits a bit. Then they gathered all their weapons, and two of them picked me up under the arms like a French lady and carried me through the streets of Madrid.

The people who saw me said, "They're taking that man to jail."

And others said, "No, it's to the hospital."

And none of them were right. I was confused and stunned. I didn't know what to do or what to say. Because if I cried for help, they would complain about me to the law, and I was more afraid of that than death. It was impossible for me to run away, not only because of the beating they had given me, but because I was surrounded by the father, sons, and relatives-- eight or nine of them had gotten together for the enterprise. They were walking along, like Saint George, armed to the teeth.

We crossed streets and passed by alleys without my knowing where I was or where I was taking them. We reached the Sol Gate, and I saw a gallant young fellow coming up one of the streets that led to it, prancing on tiptoe, his cape under his arm, with a huge glove in one hand and a carnation in the other, swinging his arms like he was the first cousin of the Duke of Infantado. He was moving his hands and swaying back and forth. I recognized him immediately: it was my master, the squire, who had stolen my clothes in Murcia. I don't doubt for a minute but that some saint put him there for me (because there wasn't one left in the litany that I hadn't called on). When I saw opportunity knocking, I grabbed it by the head and decided to kill two birds with one stone--taking vengeance on that bragger and freeing myself from those hangmen.

So I said to them, "Look! That libertine who stole your honor is coming this way, and he's changed his clothes."

They were blind with rage, and without further ado they asked me which one he was. I pointed him out. They fell on him, and grabbing him by the collar, they threw him to the ground and kicked, trampled, and clouted him. One of the boys, a brother of the girl, wanted to run him through with his sword, but his father stopped him and called the law officers over, and they put shackles on the squire. When I saw all the turmoil and everyone busy, I made myself scarce and hid as well as I could.

My good squire had recognized me, and thinking that those were relatives of mine demanding my clothes back, he said, "Let me go, let me go! I'll pay you enough for two suits of clothes!"

But they stopped up his mouth with their fists. Bleeding, his head pounded in, and beaten to a pulp, they took him off to jail while I left Madrid, damning my job and whoever had invented it.

XI How Lazaro Left for His Homeland and What Happened to Him on the Way

I wanted to be on my way, but my strength wasn't equal to my intentions, and so I stayed in Madrid for a few days. I didn't get along badly there because I used a pair of crutches--since I couldn't walk without them-- and I begged from door to door and from convent to convent until I had enough strength to

set out. I was quick to do it because of what I heard a beggar tell who was sitting in the sun with some others, picking off fleas.

It was the story of the trunk I've just told about, but the beggar added that the man they put in jail, thinking he was the one who had been inside the chest, had proved it wasn't him. Because at the time it had all happened he was in his room; and none of his neighbors had ever seen him wearing any other clothes than the ones he had on when they arrested him. But even at that, they had still paraded him through the streets for being a vagabond, and had banished him from Madrid. The beggar also told how that man and the maiden's relatives were looking for a baggage carrier, who had contrived the whole business, and they swore that the first one who found him would run him through until he looked like a sieve.

When I heard that, I was all eyes, and I put a patch over one of them. Then I shaved off my beard like a mock priest, and the way I looked then, I was sure that not even the mother who bore me would have recognized me. I left Madrid, intending to go to Tejares to see whether fortune would disown me if I went back to the mold. I passed by the Escorial, a building that reflects the greatness of the monarch who was having it built (it wasn't finished yet) and so much so that it can be counted among the wonders of the world, although you can't say it is a very pleasant place to have it built at, since the land is barren and mountainous. But the summer air is so nice that all you have to do is sit in the shade and you won't be bothered by the heat or the cold, and the air is very healthy.

Less than three miles from there I met a band of gypsies who had set up camp in an old country house. When they saw me from a distance they thought I was one of them because my clothes seemed to promise no less; but when I got close they saw they were mistaken. They shunned me a little because, as I saw, they were holding a conference or debate on thievery. They told me that wasn't the road to Salamanca but to Valladolid. Since my business didn't force me to go to one place instead of any other, I told them that if that's the way it was, I wanted to see that city before I went back to my own town.

One of the oldest men there asked me where I was from, and when I told him Tejares, he invited me to eat with them because we were almost neighbors: he was from Salamanca. I accepted, and afterwards they asked me to tell about myself and my life. I did (they didn't have to ask me twice), with the fewest and shortest words that such great things allowed. When I came to the part about the barrel and what happened to me at the innkeeper's place in Madrid, they burst into laughter, especially a man and woman gypsy who nearly split their sides. I began to feel ashamed, and my face turned red.

The gypsy who was my neighbor saw me blushing, and he said, "Don't be ashamed, brother. These people aren't laughing at you; your life is more deserving of admiration than laughter. And since you have told us so much about yourself, it is only right that we should repay you the same way. We will put our trust in you just as you have trusted us. And if the people here will allow me, I will tell you the reason for their laughter."

Everyone told him to go ahead because they knew he was discreet and experienced enough not to let things go too far.

"For your information, then," he continued, "those people who are laughing over there are the maiden and the priest who jumped *in puribus* when the deluge from your barrel nearly flooded them. If they want to they can tell you how the turns of fortune have brought them to their present state."

The brand new gypsy girl asked them to let her do it, capturing the benevolence of the illustrious audience, and so, with a sonorous, peaceful, and grave voice, she told her story.

"The day I left, or leaped (to be more accurate), from my father's house and they took me off to prison, they put me in a room that was darker than it was clean and that reeked more than it was decorated. Father Urbez, who is here and won't let me lie, was put in jail until he told them he was a priest. Then they immediately gave him over to the bishop, who scolded him severely for having let himself be overcome by a drop in the ocean and for having caused such a scandal. But when he promised to be more careful and watch himself so that not even the ground would know of his comings and goings, they let him loose and told him not to say mass for a month.

"I stayed in the warden's charge, and since he was a young, handsome fellow and I was not a bad-looking girl, he took special care of me. For me, jail was a palace--a garden of pleasures. My parents were indignant at my looseness but did what they could so I could get loose. But it was useless: the warden arranged things so I wouldn't escape his hands. Meanwhile the priest, who is here with us, was walking around the prison like an Irish setter, trying to get to talk to me. He was able to do it by means of a third party who was first in the bawdry business. She dressed him up like one of her maids, in a skirt and blouse, then she put a muffler over his beard, as if he had a toothache. At this interview my escape was planned.

"The next night there was a party at the house of Count Miranda, and some gypsies were going to dance at the end of it. Canil (that's the name of Reverend Urbez now) arranged for them to help him with his plans. The gypsies did everything so well that, because of their cleverness, we got the liberty we wanted and their company, too--the best on earth. The afternoon before the party I smiled at the warden more than a cat at a tripe stand, and I made more promises than a sailor in a storm. Feeling favored by them, he answered with just as many and begged me to ask him for anything and he would give it, as long as it wasn't to lose sight of me. I thanked him very much and told him that if I lost sight of him that would be the worst thing that could happen to me. Seeing that I had struck home, I begged him--since he could do it--to take me to the party that night. He thought it would be difficult, but not to go back on his promise and because the little blind archer had wounded him with an arrow, he gave his word.

"The chief constable was in love with me, too, and he had ordered all the guards, and even the warden, to take care of me and not to move me anywhere. To keep it secret, the warden dressed me up like a page in a damask green suit, trimmed in gold. The cloak was velvet of the same color, lined with yellow satin; the brimmed cap had feathers and a little diamond band. The neck was scalloped lace, the stockings were straw-colored with large, embroidered garters, the shoes were white with a perforated design, and there was a gilded sword and dagger like those made by Ayresvola.

"We came to the hall where there were large numbers of ladies and gentlemen: the men were gallant and jovial, the ladies were elegant and beautiful, and many kept their faces covered with shawls and capes. Canil was dressed like a braggadocio, and when he saw me he came up to my side, so that I was standing between him and the warden.

"The festivities began, and I saw things I won't tell about since they're beside the point. The gypsies came out to dance and do tumbling tricks. Two of them began to have words about their tumbling; one word led to another, and the first one called the other a liar. The one who had been called a liar brought his knife down on the other one's head, and so much blood began pouring out you would have thought they had killed an ox. The people there, who thought it was a joke until then, began to run around, shouting, 'Help, help!' Some law officers ran over, and everyone reached for his sword. I pulled out my own, and when I saw it in my hand I trembled at the sight of it. They grabbed the guilty man, and a man who had been put there for that purpose by the gypsies said the warden was there and would take care of him. The chief constable called the warden over to put the murderer in his hands. The warden wanted to take me with him, but he was afraid I might be recognized, and he told me to go over to a corner he pointed out and not to move from there until he came back. When I saw that that crab louse had let go of me I took hold of Father Canil's hand. He was still by my side, and we were in the street like a shot. There we found one of these gentlemen who took us to his camp.

"When the wounded man (whom every- one believed was dead) thought we must have escaped, he got to his feet and said, 'Gentlemen, the joke is over. I'm not hurt, and we did this to brighten up the party.'

"He took off his cap, and inside was an ox bladder on top of a good steel helmet. It had been filled with blood and had burst open when the knife struck it. Everyone began to laugh at the joke except the warden, who didn't like it at all. He went back to the place where he had told me to wait, and when he didn't find me there he started looking for me. He asked an old gypsy woman if she had seen a page of such and such a description, and since she was in on our game she told him she had and that she had heard him say as he was leaving, holding a man's hand, 'Let's go hide in the convent of San Felipe.'

"He quickly went after me, but it did no good because he went east and we were running to the west.

"Before we left Madrid we exchanged my clothes for these, and they gave me two hundred pieces of silver besides. I sold the diamond band for four hundred gold pieces. And when we got here I gave these gentlemen two hundred, as Canil had promised them. That's the story of how I was set free, and if Mr. Lazaro wants anything else, let him ask. We will do for him whatever the gentleman desires."

I thanked her for the courtesy, and as best I could I took my leave of them all. The good old man walked with me for a few miles. As we were walking along I asked him if those people were all gypsies born in Egypt. He told me there wasn't a damned one from Egypt in Spain: all of them there were really priests, friars, nuns, or thieves who had escaped from jail or from their convents. But the biggest scoundrels of all were the ones who had left their monasteries, exchanging the contemplative life for the active one. The old man went back to his camp, while I rode to Valladolid on the shank's mare.

XII - What Happened to Lazaro in an Inn Three Miles outside of Valladolid

What thoughts I had all along the road about my good gypsies: their way of life, their customs, the way they behaved. It really amazed me that the law let such thieves go around so freely, since everyone knows that their life involves nothing but stealing. Theirs is an asylum--a shelter for thieves, a congregation of apostates, and a school for evil. I was especially astonished that friars would leave a life of rumination to follow the one of ruination and fatigue of the gypsies. I wouldn't have believed what the gypsy told me if he hadn't shown me a gypsy man and woman a mile from the camp, behind the walls of a shelter: he was broad-shouldered, and she was plump. He wasn't sunburned, and she wasn't tanned by harsh weather. One of them was singing a verse from the psalms of David, and the other was answering with another verse. The good old man told me that they were a friar and a nun who had come to his congregation not more than a week ago, wanting to profess a more austere life.

I came to an inn three miles from Valladolid, and I saw the old lady from Madrid,
along with the young maiden of yore, sitting in
the doorway. A gallant young fellow came out to
call them in to eat. They didn't recognize me because of my good disguise: my patch still over
one eye and my clothes worn in the roguish
style. But I knew I was the Lazaro who had
come out of the tomb that had been so harsh on
me. I went up to them to see if they would give
me anything. But they couldn't because they
didn't have anything for themselves. The young
man who served as their steward was so generous that, for himself, his sweetheart, and the old
bawd, he'd had a tiny bit of pork liver prepared
with a sauce. I could have shoveled down everything on the plate in less than two mouthfuls.
The bread was as black as the tablecloth, and
that looked like a penitent's tunic or a rag for
cleaning stoves.

"Eat, my dove," the gentleman said.
"This meal is fit for a prince."

The go-between ate without a word so as
not to lose any time and because she saw there
wasn't enough for all of them. They began to
clean up the plate with such gusto that they re-
moved the finish. When the poor, sad meal was
over--and it had made them more hungry than
full--the gentle lover made excuses by saying the
inn didn't have much food.

When I saw they didn't have anything for me, I asked the innkeeper what there was to eat. He told me, "It depends how much you want to pay." He wanted to give me a few chitterlings. I asked him if he had anything else. He offered me a quarter of kid that the lover hadn't wanted because it was too expensive. I wanted to impress them, so I told him to give it to me. I sat down with it at the end of the table, and their stares were a sight to behold. With each mouthful I swallowed six eyes, because those of the lover, the girl, and the bawd were fastened on what I was eating.

"What's going on?" asked the maiden. "That poor man is eating a quarter of kid, and there was nothing for us but a poor piece of fried liver."

The young fellow answered that he had asked the innkeeper for some partridges, capons or hens, and that he had told him he didn't have anything else to offer. I knew the truth of the matter--that he had put them on that diet because he didn't want to pay or couldn't, but I decided to eat and keep quiet. The kid was like a magnet. Without warning, I found all three of them hovering over my plate.

The brazen-faced little bitch picked up a piece and said, "With your permission, brother." But before she had it, she had the piece in her mouth.

The old woman said, "Don't steal his meal from this poor sinner."

"I'm not stealing it," she answered. "I intend to pay him for it very well."

And in the same breath she began to eat so fast and furiously that it looked like she hadn't eaten in six days. The old woman took a bite

to see how it tasted.

"Is it really that good?" said the young man. And he filled his mouth with an enormous piece. When I saw that they were going too far, I picked up everything on the plate and stuck it in my mouth. It was so big that it couldn't go down or up.

While I was in this struggle, two armed men came riding up to the door of the inn, wearing vests and helmets and carrying shields. Each of them had one musket at his side and another on the saddle. They dismounted and gave their mules to a foot servant. They asked the innkeeper if there was anything to eat. He told them he had a good supply of food, and if they liked they could go into the hall while he was preparing it. The old woman had gone over to the door when she heard the noise, and she came back with her hands over her face, bowing as much as a novice monk. She spoke with a wee, tiny voice and was laboriously twisting back and forth like she was going into labor.

As softly and well as she could, she said, "We're lost. Clara's brothers (Clara was the maiden's name) are outside."

The girl began to pull and tear at her hair, hitting herself so hard it was like she was possessed. The young man was courageous, and he consoled her, telling her not to worry, that he could handle everything. I was all ears, with my mouth full of kid, and when I heard that those braggers were there I thought I was going to die of fear. And I would have, too, but since my gullet was closed off, my soul didn't find the door standing open, and it went back down.

The two Cids came in, and as soon as they saw their sister and the bawd they shouted, "Here they are! At last we have them. Now they'll die!"

I was so frightened by their shouts that I fell to the floor, and when I hit I ejected the goat that was choking me. The two women got behind the young man like chicks under a hen's wing running from a hawk. Brave and graceful, he pulled out his sword and went at the brothers so furiously that their fright turned them into statues. The words froze in their mouths, and the swords in their sheaths. The young man asked them what they wanted or what they were looking for, and as he was talking he grabbed one of them and took away his sword. Then he pointed this sword at his eyes, while he held his own sword at the other one's eyes. At every movement he made with the swords, they trembled like leaves. When the old woman and the sister saw the two Rolands so subdued, they went up and disarmed them. The innkeeper came in at the noise we were all making (I had gotten up and had one of them by the beard).

It all seemed to me like the gentle bulls in my town: boys, when they see them, run away; but they gradually get more and more daring, and when they see they aren't as fierce as they look, they lose all their fear and go right up and throw all kinds of garbage on them. When I saw that those scarecrows weren't as ferocious as they looked, I plucked up my courage and attacked them more bravely than my earlier terror had allowed.

"What's this?" asked the innkeeper. "Who dares to cause such an uproar in my house?"

The women, the gentleman, and I began shouting that they were thieves who had been following us to rob us. When the innkeeper saw them without any weapons, and at our mercy, he said, "Thieves in my house!"

He grabbed hold of them and helped us put them in a cellar, not listening to one word of their protests. Their servant came back from feeding the mules, and he asked where his masters were: the innkeeper put him in with them. He took their bags, their saddle cushions, and their portmanteaus and locked them up, and he gave us the weapons as if they belonged to him. He didn't charge us for the food so that we would sign a lawsuit he had drawn up against them. He said he was a minister of the Inquisition, and as a law officer in that district, he was condemning the three of them to the galleys for the rest of their lives, and to be whipped two hundred times around the inn. They appealed to the Chancery of Valladolid, and the good innkeeper and three of his servants took them there.

When the poor fellows thought they were before the judges, they found themselves before the Inquisitors, because the sly innkeeper had put down on the record some words they had spoken against the officials of the Holy Inquisition (an unpardonable crime). They put the brothers in dark jail cells, and they couldn't write their father or ask anyone to help them the way they had thought they could.

And there we will leave them, well guarded, to get back to our innkeeper, because we met him on the road. He told us that the Inquisitors had commanded him to have the witnesses who had signed the lawsuit appear before them. But, as a friend, he was advising us to go into hiding. The young maiden gave him a ring from her finger, begging him to arrange things so we wouldn't have to appear. He promised he would. But the thief said this to make us leave, so that if they wanted to hear witnesses they wouldn't discover his chicanery (and it wasn't his first).

In two weeks Valladolid was the scene of an *auto de fe*, and I saw the three poor devils come out with other penitents, with gags in their mouths, as blasphemers who had dared speak against the ministers of the Holy Inquisition--a group of people as saintly and perfect as the justice they deal out. All three of them were wearing pointed hats and sanbenitos, and written on them were their crimes and the sentences they had been given. I was sorry to see that poor foot servant paying for something he hadn't done. But I didn't feel as much pity for the other two because they'd had so little on me. The innkeeper's sentence was carried out, with the addition of three hundred lashes apiece, so they were given five hundred and sent to the galleys where their fierce bravado melted away.

I sought out my fortune. Many times, on the street of Magdalena, I ran into my two women friends. But they never recognized me or were aware that I knew them. After a few days I saw the missionary-minded young maiden in the prisoners' cells where she earned enough to maintain her affair and herself. The old woman carried on her business in that city.

XIII - How Lazaro Was a Squire for Seven Women at One Time

I reached Valladolid with six silver pieces in my purse because the people who saw me looking so skinny and pale gave me money with open hands, and I didn't take it with closed ones. I went straight to the clothing store, and for four silver coins and a twenty-copper piece I bought a long baize cloak, worn out, torn and unraveled, that had belonged to a Portuguese. With that, and a high, wide-brimmed hat like a Franciscan monk's that I bought for half a silver piece, and with a cane in my hand, I took a stroll around.

People who saw me mocked me. Everyone had a different name for me. Some of them called me a tavern philosopher. Others said, "There goes Saint Peter, all dressed up for his feast day."

And still others: "Oh, Mr. Portugee, would you like some polish for your boots?"

And somebody even said I must be a quack doctor's ghost. I closed my ears like a shopkeeper and walked right past.

After I had gone down a few streets I came upon a woman dressed in a full skirt, with very elegant shoes. She also had on a silk veil that came down to her bosom and had her hand on a little boy's head. She asked me if I knew of any squires around there. I answered that I was the only one I knew of and that if she liked she could use me as her own. It was all arranged in the twinkling of an eye. She promised me sixty coppers for my meals and wages. I took the job and offered her my arm. I threw away the cane because I didn't need it anymore, and I was only using it to appear sickly and move people to pity. She sent the child home, telling him to have the maid set the table and get dinner ready. For more than two hours she took me from pillar to post, up one street and down another.

The lady told me that when she got to the first house we were going to stop at, I was to go up to the house first and ask for the master or mistress of the house, and say, "My lady, Juana Perez (that was her name), is here and would like to pay her respects."

She also told me that whenever I was with her and she stopped anywhere, I was always to take off my hat. I told her I knew what a servant's duties were, and I would carry them out.

I really wanted to see my new mistress's face, but she kept her veil over it, and I couldn't. She told me she wouldn't be able to keep me by herself but that she would arrange for some ladies who were neighbors of hers to use me, and between them they would give me the money she had promised. And meanwhile, until they all agreed--which wouldn't take long--she would give me her share. She asked me if I had a place to sleep. I told her I didn't.

"I'll get you one," she said. "My husband is a tailor, and you can sleep with his apprentices. You couldn't find a better- paying job in the whole city," she continued, "because in three days you'll have six ladies, and each of them will give you ten coppers."

I was nearly dumbstruck to see the pomposity of that woman who appeared to be, at the very least, the wife of a privileged gentleman or of some wealthy citizen. I was also astonished to see that I would have to serve seven mistresses to earn seventy poor coppers a day. But I thought that anything was better than nothing, and it wasn't hard work. That was something I fled from like the Devil, because I was always more for eating cabbage and garlic without working than for working to eat capons and hens.

When we came to her house, she gave me the veil and the shoes to give to the maid, and I saw what I was longing for. The young woman didn't look bad at all to me: she was a sprightly brunette, with a nice figure. The only thing I didn't like was that her face gleamed like a glazed earthen pot.

She gave me the ten coppers and told me to come back two times every day--at eight in the morning and three in the afternoon-- to see if she wanted to go out. I went to a pastry shop, and with a ten-copper piece of pie I put an end to my day's wages. I spent the rest of the day like a chameleon because I had spent the money I'd begged along the road. I didn't dare go begging anymore because if my mistress heard about it she would eat me alive.

I went to her house at three o'clock; she told me she didn't want to go out, but she warned me that from then on she wouldn't pay me on the days she didn't go out, and that if she only went out once a day she would give me five coppers and no more. But she said that since she was giving me a place to sleep, she expected to be served before all the others, and she wanted me to call myself her servant. For the sort of bed it was, she deserved that and even more. She made me sleep with the apprentices on a large table without a damned thing to cover us but a worn-out blanket.

I spent two days on the miserable food that I could afford with ten coppers. Then the wife of a tanner joined the fraternity, and she haggled over the ten coppers for more than an hour. Finally, after five days, I had seven mistresses, and my wages were seventy coppers. I began to eat splendidly: the wine I drank wasn't the worst, but it wasn't the best either (I didn't want to overreach my hand and have it lopped off). The five other women were the wife of a constable, a gardener's wife, the niece (or so she said) of a chaplain in the Discalced order, a good-looking, sprightly girl, and a tripe merchant. This last woman I liked best because whenever she gave me the ten coppers she invited me to have some tripe soup, and before I left her house I would have guzzled down three or four bowlsful.

So I was living as content as could be. The last mistress was a devout woman: I had more to do with her than with the others because all she ever did was visit with friars, and when she was alone with them she was in her glory. Her house was like a beehive: some coming, others going, and they all came with their sleeves stuffed with things for her. For me, so I would be a faithful secretary, they brought some pieces of meat from their meals, which they put in their sleeves. I have never in my life seen a more hypocritical woman than she was. When she walked down the street she never took her eyes off the ground; her rosary was always in her hand, and she would always be praying on it in the streets. Every woman who knew her begged her to pray to God for them since her prayers were so acceptable to Him. She told them she was a great

sinner (and that was no lie), but she was lying
with the truth.

Each of my mistresses had her own special time for me to come. When one of them said
she didn't want to go out, I went to the next
one's house, until I finished my rounds. They

told me what time to come back for them and without fail, because if I (sinner that I am) was even a little bit late, the lady would insult me in front of everyone she visited, and she would threaten me, saying that if I kept being so careless she would get another squire who was more diligent, careful, and punctual. Anyone hearing her shout and threaten me so haughtily undoubtedly thought she was paying me two pieces of silver every day and a salary of three hundred silver pieces a year besides. When my mistresses walked down the street each one looked like the wife of the judge over all Castile, or at least, of a judge of the Chancery.

One day it happened that the chaplain's niece and the constable's wife met in a church, and both of them wanted to go home at the same time. The quarrel about which one I would take home first was so loud that it was as though we were in jail. They grabbed hold of me and pulled--one at one side and one at the other--so fiercely that they tore my cloak to shreds. And there I stood, stark naked, because I didn't have a damned thing under it but some ragged underwear that looked like a fish net. The people who saw the fish hook peeping out from the torn underwear laughed their heads off. The church was like a tavern: some were making fun of poor Lazaro; others were listening to the two women dig up their grandparents. I was in such a hurry to gather up the pieces of my cloak that had fallen in their ripeness that I didn't get a chance to listen to what they were saying. I only heard the widow say, 'Where does this whore get all her pride? Yesterday she was a water girl, and today she wears taffeta dresses at the expense of the souls in purgatory.

The other woman answered, "This one, the old gossip, got her black frocks at bargain prices from those who pay with a *Deo Gratias*, or a 'be charitable in God's name.' And if I was a water girl yesterday, she's a hot-air merchant today."

The people there separated the women because they had begun to pull each other's hair. I finished picking up the pieces of my poor cloak, and I asked a devout woman there for two pins. Then I fixed it as well as I could and covered up my private parts.

I left them quarreling and went to the tailor's wife's house. She had told me to be there at eleven because she had to go to dinner at a friend's house. When she saw how ragged I looked, she shouted at me, "Do you think you're going to earn my money and escort me like a picaro? I could have another squire with stylish trousers, breeches, a cape and hat, for less than I pay you. And you're always getting drunk on what I give you."

What do you mean, getting drunk? I thought to myself. With seventy coppers that I make a day, at most? And many days my mistresses don't even leave their houses just so that they won't have to pay me a cent. The tailor's wife had them stitch together the pieces of my cloak, and they were in such a hurry that they put some of the pieces on top that belonged on the bottom. And that's the way I went with her.

XIV - Where Lazaro Tells What Happened to Him at a Dinner

We went flying along like a friar who has been invited out to dinner because the lady was afraid there wouldn't be enough left for her. We reached her friend's house, and inside were other women who had been invited, too. They asked my mistress if I would be able to guard the door; she told them I could. They said to me, "Stay here, brother. Today you'll eat like a king."

Many gallant young men came, each one pulling something out of his pocket: this one a partridge, that one a hen; one took out a rabbit, another one a couple of pigeons; this one a little mutton, that one a piece of loin; and someone brought out sausage or blackpudding. One of them even took out a pie worth a silver piece, wrapped up in his handkerchief. They gave it to the cook, and in the meantime they were frolicking around with the ladies, romping with them like donkeys in a new field of rye. It isn't right for me to tell what happened there or for the reader to even imagine it.

After these rituals there came the victuals. The ladies ate the *Aves*, and the young men drank the *ite misa est*. Everything left on

225

the table the ladies wrapped in their handker-
chiefs and put in their pockets. Then the men
pulled the dessert out of theirs: some, apples;
others, cheese; some, olives; and one of them,
who was the cock of the walk and the one who
was fooling with the tailor's wife, brought out a
half-pound of candied fruit. I really liked that
way of keeping your meal so close, in case you
need it. And I decided right then that I would
put three or four pockets on the first pair of
pants God would give me, and one of them
would be of good leather, sewn up well enough
to pour soup into. Because if those gentlemen
who were so rich and important brought everything in their pockets and the ladies carried
things that were cooked in theirs, I--who was
only a whore's squire--could do it, too.

We servants went to eat, and there wasn't
a damned thing left for us but soup and bread
sops, and I was amazed to see that those ladies
hadn't stuck that up their sleeves. We had barely
begun when we heard a tremendous uproar in
the hall where our masters were: they were re-
ferring to their mothers and discussing what sort
of men their fathers had been. They left off talking and started swinging, and since variety is
necessary in everything, there was hitting, slap-
ping, pinching, kicking, and biting. They were
grabbing one another's hair and pulling it out;
they pounded each other so much you would

think they were village boys in a religious procession. As far as I could find out, the quarrel broke out because some of the men didn't want to give or pay those women anything: they said that what the women had eaten was enough.

It happened that some law officers were coming up the street, and they heard the noise and knocked on the door and called out, "Open up, in the name of the law!"

When they heard this, some of the people inside ran one way, and others another way. Some left behind their cloaks, and others their swords, one left her shoes, another her veil. So they all disappeared, and each one hid as best he could. I had no reason to run away, so I stood there, and since I was the doorman, I opened the door so they wouldn't accuse me of resisting the law. The first officer who came in grabbed me by the collar and said I was under arrest. When they had me in their hands, they locked the door and went looking for the people who had been making all the noise. There was no bedroom, dressing room, basement, wine cellar, attic, or privy they didn't look in.

Since the officers didn't find anyone, they took my statement. I confessed from A to Z about everyone at the gathering and what they had done. The officers were amazed, since there were as many as I'd said, that not one of them had turned up. To tell the truth, I was amazed, too, because there had been twelve men and six women. Simple as I was, I told them (and I really believed it) that I thought all the people who had been there and made that noise were goblins. They laughed at me, and the constable asked his men who had been to the wine cellar if they'd looked everywhere carefully. They said they had, but not satisfied with this, he made them light a torch, and when they went in the door they saw a cask rolling around. The officers were terrified, and they started to run away, crying, "For God's sake, that fellow was right; there are nothing but spooks here!"

The constable was shrewder, and he stopped the officers, saying he wasn't afraid of the Devil himself. Then he went over to the cask and took off the lid, and inside he found a man and a woman. I don't want to tell how he found them so I won't offend the pure ears of the wholesome, high-minded reader. I will only say that the violence of their movements had made the cask roll around and was the cause of their misfortune and of showing in public what they were doing in private.

The officers pulled them out: he looked like Cupid with his arrow, and she like Venus with her quiver. Both of them were as naked as the day they were born because, when the officers had knocked, they were in bed, kissing the holy relics, and with the alarm they didn't have a chance to pick up their clothes. And, to hide, they had climbed into that empty cask, where they continued their devout exercise.

Everyone stood there, agape at the beauty of these two. Then they threw two cloaks over them and put them in the custody of two officers, and they started looking for the others. The constable discovered a large earthen jug filled with oil, and inside he found a man fully dressed and up to his chest in the oil. As soon as they saw him he tried to jump out, but he didn't do it so agilely that the jug and he both didn't tip over. The oil flew out and covered the officers from head to foot, staining them without any respect. They stood there cursing the job and the whore who taught it to them. The oiled man saw that instead of grabbing him they were avoiding him like the plague, and he began to run away.

The constable shouted, "Stop him! Stop him!" But they all made room for him to go past. He went out a back door, pissing oil. What he wrung from his clothes he used to light the lamp of Our Lady of Afflictions for more than a month.

The law officers stood there, bathed in oil, and cursing whoever had brought them to the place. And so was I, because they said I was the pander and they were going to tar and feather me. They went out like fritters from the frying pan, leaving a trail wherever they walked. They were so irate that they swore to God and to the four holy Gospels that they would hang everyone they found. We prisoners trembled. They went over to the storeroom to look for the others. They went in, and from the top of a door a bag of flour was poured down on them, blinding them all.

They shouted, "Stop, in the name of the law!"

If they tried to open their eyes, they were immediately closed up with flour and water. The men holding us let go so they could help the constable who was yelling like a madman. They had hardly gotten inside when their eyes were covered with flour and water, too. They were wandering around like they were playing blindman's bluff, bumping into and clouting each other so much they broke their jaws and teeth.

When we saw that the officers were done in, we threw ourselves on them, and they attacked each other so wildly that they fell, exhausted, to the floor while blows and kicks rained and hailed down on top of them. Finally, they didn't shout or move any more than dead men. If one of them tried to open his mouth, it was immediately filled with flour and stuffed like a capon at a poultry farm. We bound their hands and feet and carried them along like hogs to the wine cellar. We threw them in the oil like fish to be fried, and they squirmed around like pigs in a mire. Then we locked up the doors, and we all went home.

The owner of that one had been in the country, and when he came back he found the doors locked and that no one answered when he called. A niece of his had loaned out his house for that feast, and she had gone back to her father's, afraid of what her uncle would do. The man had the doors unlocked, and when he saw his house sown with flour and anointed with oil, he flew into a rage and began shouting like a drunkard. He went to the wine cellar and found his oil spilled all over and the law officers wallowing in it. He was so angry to see his home devastated that he picked up a cudgel and hammered away on the constable and the officers, leaving them half dead. He called his neighbors over, and they helped drag them out to the street, and there boys threw mud, garbage, and filth on the officers and the constable. They were so full of flour no one recognized them. When they came to and found themselves in the street, free, they took to their heels. Then people could very well have said, "Stop the name of the law- -it's running away!"

They left behind their cloaks, swords, and daggers and didn't dare go back for them so that no one would find out what had happened.

The owner of the house kept everything that was left behind as compensation for the damage that had been done. When I came out, ready to leave, I found a cloak that wasn't at all bad, and I took it and left mine there. I thanked God I had come out ahead this time (something new for me), since I was always getting the short end of things. I went to the house of the tailor's wife. I found the house in an uproar, and the tailor, her husband, was thrashing her with a stick for having come back alone without her veil or shoes and for running down the street with more than a hundred boys after her. I got there at just the right time because, as soon as the tailor saw me, he left his wife and sailed into me with a blow that finished off the few teeth I still had. Then he kicked me ten or twelve times in the belly, and that made me throw up what little I had eaten.

"You damned pimp!" he cried. "You mean you're not ashamed to come back to my house? I'll give you enough payment to settle every score--past and present."

He called his servants, and they brought a blanket and tossed me in it to their own pleasure, which was my grief. They left me for dead and laid me out on a bench like that. It was nighttime when I recovered my senses, and I tried to get up and walk. But I fell to the ground and broke an arm. The next morning I made my way to the door of a church, little by little, and

there I begged with a pitiful voice from the people going in.

XV - *How Lazaro Became a Hermit*

Stretched out at the door of the church and reviewing my past life, I thought over the misery I had gone through from the day I began to serve the blind man down to the present. And I came to the conclusion that even if a man always rises early, that doesn't make dawn come any earlier, and if you work hard, that won't necessarily make you rich. And there's a saying that goes like this: "The early riser fails where God's help succeeds." I put myself in His hands so that the end would be better than the beginning and the middle had been.

A venerable, white-bearded hermit was next to me with his staff and a rosary in his hand, and at the end of the rosary hung a skull the size of a rabbit's.

When the good Father saw me in such misery he began to console me with kind, soft words, and he asked me where I was from and what had happened to bring me to such a pitiful state. I told him very briefly the long process of my bitter pilgrimage. He was astonished by what I said and showed his pity on me by inviting me to his hermitage. I accepted the invitation, and as well as I could (which wasn't painlessly) I reached the oratory with him, a few miles from there, in the side of a hill. Attached to it was a little house with a bedroom and a bed. In the patio was a cistern with fresh water, and it was used to water a garden--neater and better cared for than it was large.

"I have been living here," said the good old man, "for twenty years, apart from the commotion and anxiety of man. This, brother, is earthly paradise. Here I contemplate both divine and human matters. Here I fast when I am well fed, and I eat when I am hungry. Here I stay awake when I can't sleep, and I sleep when I grow tired. Here I have solitude when no one is with me, and I have company when I am not alone. Here I sing when I am happy, and I cry when I am sad. Here I work when I'm not idle, and I am idle when I don't work. Here I think about my past bad life, and I contemplate the good one I have now. And, finally, here nothing is known, and the knowledge of all things is attained."

I rejoiced in my heart to listen to the cunning hermit, and I begged him to tell me about hermit life, since it seemed to be the best in the world.

"What do you mean, the best?" he answered. "Only a person who has enjoyed it can know how good it really is. But we don't have time to speak further of this because it's time to

have dinner."

I begged him to heal my arm because it hurt very much. He did it so easily that from then on it never bothered me. We ate like kings and drank like Germans. After the meal was

over, and while we were taking an afternoon
nap, my good hermit began to shout, "I'm dying!
I'm dying!"

I got up and saw that he looked like he
was about to breathe his last. And I asked him if
he really was dying.

"Yes, yes, yes!" he answered.

And still repeating "yes," he died an hour
later.

But at the time he told me that, I was very
upset. I realized that if the man died without

witnesses, people might say I had killed him, and it would cost me the life I had kept up with such hard work. And it wouldn't take very weighty witnesses for that because I looked more like a robber than an honest man. I immediately ran out of the hermitage to see if anyone was around who could be a witness to the old man's death. I looked everywhere and saw a flock of sheep nearby. I quickly (although painfully because of the beating I had gotten in the tailor skirmish) went toward it. I found six or seven shepherds and four or five shepherdesses resting in the shade of some willows, next to a shining, clear spring. The men were playing instruments and the women were singing. Some were capering, others were dancing. One of the men was holding a woman's hand, another was resting with his head on a woman's lap. And they were spending the heat of the day wooing each other with sweet words.

I ran up to them, terrified, and begged them to come with me right away because the old hermit was dying. Some of them came along while others stayed behind to watch over the sheep. They went into the hermitage and asked the good hermit if he was approaching death. He said, "Yes" (but that was a lie because he wasn't going anywhere: it was death that was approaching him, and against his will). When I saw that he was still in his rut about saying yes, I asked him if he wanted those shepherds to be witnesses for his last will and testament. He answered, "Yes."

I asked him if he was leaving me as his sole and lawful heir. He said, "Yes." I went on,

asking if he acknowledged and confessed that everything he possessed or might possess he was leaving to me for services and other things he had received from me. Again he said, "Yes."

I was wishing that would be the last noise he'd make, but I saw that he still had a little breath left in him, and, so that he wouldn't do me any harm with it, I went on with my questions and had one of the shepherds write down everything he said. The shepherd wrote on a wall with a piece of coal since we didn't have an ink-well or a pen.

I asked him if he wanted that shepherd to sign for him since he was in no position to do it himself, and he died, saying, "Yes, yes, yes."

We went ahead and buried him: we dug a grave in his garden (and did it all very quickly because I was afraid he might come back to life). I invited the shepherds to have something to eat; they didn't want to because it was time to feed their sheep. They went away, giving me their condolences.

I locked the door of the hermitage and walked all around the inside. I found a huge jug of good wine, another one full of oil, and two crocks of honey. He had two sides of bacon, a good quantity of jerked beef, and some dried fruit. I liked all of this very much, but it wasn't what I was looking for. I found his chests full of linens, and in the corner of one of them was a woman's dress. This surprised me, but what surprised me even more was that such a well-provided man wouldn't have any money. I went to the grave to ask him where he had put it.

It seemed to me that after I had asked him he answered: "You stupid fellow. Do you think that living out here in the country the way I do, at the mercy of thieves and bandits, I would keep it in a coffer where I'd be in danger of losing what I loved more than my own life?"

It was as if I had really heard this inspiration from his mouth, and it made me look around in every corner. But when I didn't find anything, I thought: If I were going to hide money here so no one else could find it, where would I put it? And I said to myself: In that altar. I went over to it and took the frontpiece of the altar off the pedestal, which was made of mud and clay. On one side I saw a crack that a silver coin could fit into. My blood started humming, and my heart began to flutter. I picked up a spade, and in less than two clouts I had half the altar on the ground, and I discovered the relics that were buried there. I found a jar full of coins. I counted them, and there were six hundred silver pieces. I was so overjoyed at the discovery that I

thought I would die. I took the money out of
there and dug a hole outside the hermitage
where I buried it so that if they turned me out of
there I would have what I loved most outside.

When this was done I put on the hermit's
garb and went into town to tell the prior of the
brotherhood what had happened. But first I
didn't forget to put the altar back the way it had
been before. I found all the members of the
brotherhood that the hermitage depended on
together there. The hermitage was dedicated to
Saint Lazarus, and I thought that was a good
sign for me. The members saw that I was already gray-haired and of an exemplary appear-

ance, which is the most important part of positions like this. There was, however, one difficulty, and that was that I didn't have a beard. I had sheared it off such a short time before that it hadn't yet sprung back. But even with this, seeing by the shepherds' story that the dead man had left me as his heir, they turned the hermitage over to me.

About this business of beards, I remember what a friar told me once: In his order, and even in the most reformed orders, they wouldn't make anyone a Superior unless he had a good beard. So it happened that some of them who were very capable of being in that position were excluded, and others who were woolly were given the position (as if good administration depended on hair and not on mature, capable understanding).

They warned me to live with the virtuous character and good reputation my predecessor had had, which was so great that everyone thought him a saint. I promised them I would live like a Hercules. They advised me to beg for alms only on Tuesdays and Saturdays because if I did it any other day the friars would punish me. I promised to do whatever they ordered me, and I especially didn't want to make enemies of them because I had previously experienced the taste of their hands. I began to beg for alms from door to door, with a low, humble, devout tone, the

way I had learned in the blind man's school. I didn't do this because I was in need, but because it's the beggar's character that the more they have the more they ask for and the more pleasure they get from doing it. The people who heard me calling, "Alms for the candles of Saint Lazarus," and didn't recognize my voice, came out their doors and were astonished when they saw me. They asked me where Father Anselmo was (that was the name of the good old fellow). I told them he had died.

Some said, "May he rest in peace, he was such a good man

Others said, "His soul is in the glory of God."

And some, "God bless the man whose life was like his: he ate nothing warm for six years."

And others, "He lived on bread and water."

Some of the foolish pious women got down on their knees and called on the name of Father Anselmo. One asked me what I had done with his garb. I told her I was wearing it. She took out some scissors, and without saying what she wanted she began to cut a piece from the first part she found, which was the crotch. When I saw her going after that part, I started to shout because I thought she was trying to castrate me.

When she saw how upset I was, she said, "Don't worry, brother. I want some relics from that blessed man, and I'll pay you for the damage to your robe."

"Oh," some said, "before six months are up they are certain to canonize him because he's performed so many miracles."

So many people came to see his grave that the house was always full, so I had to move the grave out to a shelter in front of the hermitage. From then on I didn't beg alms for the candles of Saint Lazarus, but for the blessed Father Anselmo. I have never understood this business of begging alms to light the candles of saints. But I don't want to continue on this note

because it will sound bad. I wasn't at all interested in going to the city because I had everything I wanted at the hermitage. But, so no one
could say I was rich and that's why I didn't go
out begging alms, I went the next day, and there
something happened to me that you'll find out if
you read:

XVI - *How Lazaro Decided to Marry Again*

Good fortune has more value than horse or mule; for an unlucky man a sow will bear mongrels. Many times we see men rise from the dust of the earth, and without knowing how, they find themselves rich, honored, feared, and held in esteem. If you ask: Is this man wise? They'll tell you: Like a mule. Is he discreet? Like an ass. Does he have any good qualities? Those of a dunce. Well, how did he become so wealthy? They'll answer: It was the work of fortune.

Other people, on the contrary, who are discreet, wise, prudent, with many good qualities, capable of ruling a kingdom, find themselves beaten down, cast aside, poor, and made into a rag for the whole world. If you ask why, they'll tell you misfortune is always following them.

And I think it was misfortune that was always pursuing and persecuting me, giving the world a sample and example of what it could do. Because since the world was made there has never been a man attacked so much by this damned fortune as I was.

I was going down a street, begging alms for Saint Lazarus as usual, because in the city I didn't beg for the blessed Anselmo-- that was only for the naive and ignorant who came to touch the rosary at his grave, where they said many miracles took place. I went up to a door, and giving my usual cry I heard some people call me from a stairway, "Why don't you come up, Father? Come on, come on, what are you doing,

staying down there?"

I started to climb the stairs, which were a little dark, and halfway up some women clasped me about the neck; others held onto my hands and stuck theirs in my pockets And since we were in the dark, when one of the women reached for my pocket she hit upon my locket.

She gave a cry, and said, 'What's this?"

I answered, "A little bird that will come out if you touch it."

They all asked why they hadn't seen me for a week. When we reached the top of the stairs they saw me in the light from the windows, and they stood there looking at each other like wooden puppets. Then they burst out laughing and laughed so hard I wondered if they would ever stop. None of them could talk. The first to speak was a little boy who said, "That isn't Daddy."

After those bursts of laughter had subsided a little, the women (there were four of them) asked me what saint I was begging alms for. I told them for Saint Lazarus.

"Why are you begging for him?" they asked. "Isn't Father Anselmo feeling well?"

"Well?" I answered. "He doesn't feel bad at all because a week ago he died."

When they heard that, they burst into tears, and if the laughter had been loud before, their wailing was even louder. Some of them screamed, others pulled their hair, and with all of them carrying on together, their music was as grating as a choir of hoarse nuns.

One of them said, "What will I do. Oh, me! Here I am without a husband, without protection, without consolation. Where will I go? Who will help me? What bitter news! What a misfortune!"

Another was lamenting with these words: "Oh, my son-in-law and my lord! How could you leave without saying good-by? Oh, my little grandchildren, now you are orphans, abandoned! Where is your good father?"

The children were carrying the soprano of that unharmonious music. They were all crying and shouting, and there was nothing but weeping and wailing. When the water of that great deluge let up a little they asked me how and what he had died from. I told them about it and about the will he had made, leaving me as his lawful heir and successor. And then it all started. The tears turned into rage, their wails into curses, and their sighs into threats.

"You're a thief, and you killed him to rob him, but you won't get away with it," said the youngest girl. "That hermit was my husband, and these three children are his, and if you don't give us all his property, we'll have you hanged. And if the law doesn't do it there are swords and daggers to kill you a thousand times if you had a thousand lives."

I told them there were reliable witnesses there when he'd made his will.

"That's a pack of lies," they said. "Because the day you say he died, he was here, and he told us he didn't have any company."

When I realized that he hadn't given his will to a notary, and that those women were threatening me, along with the experience I'd had with the law and with lawsuits, I decided to be courteous to them. I wanted to try to get hold of what I would lose if it came into the hands of the law. Besides, the new widow's tears had touched my heart. So I told them to calm down, they wouldn't lose anything with me; that if I had accepted the inheritance, it was only because I didn't know the dead man was married-- in fact, I had never heard of hermits being married.

Putting aside all their sadness and melancholy, they began to laugh, saying that it was easy to see that I was new and inexperienced in that position since I didn't know that when people talked about solitary hermits they didn't mean they had to give up the company of women. In fact, there wasn't one who didn't have at least one woman to spend some time with after he was through contemplating, and together they would engage in active exercises--so sometimes he would imitate Martha and other times Mary. Because they were people who had a better understanding of the will of God they knew that He doesn't want man to be alone. So, like obedient sons, they have one or two women they maintain, even if it is by alms.

"And this one was especially obedient because he maintained four: this poor widow, me (her mother), these two (her sisters), and these three children who are his sons (or, at least, he considered them his)."

Then the woman they called his wife said she didn't want them to call her the widow of that rotten old carcass who hadn't remembered her the day he died, and that she would swear those children weren't his, and from then on she was renouncing the marriage contract.

"What is that marriage contract?" I asked.

The mother said, "The marriage contract I drew up when my daughter married that ungrateful wretch was this.... But before I tell that, I'll have to give you the background.

"I was living in a village called Duennas, twenty miles from here. I was left with these three daughters from three different fathers who were, as near as I can figure out, a monk, an abbot, and a priest (I have always been devoted to the Church). I came to this city to live, to get away from all the gossiping that always goes on in small towns. Everyone called me the ecclesiastical widow because, unfortunately, all three men had died. And even though others came to take their place, they were only mediocre men of lower positions, and not being content with the sheep, they went after the young lambs.

"Well, when I saw the obvious danger we were in and that what we earned wouldn't make us rich, I called a halt and set up my camp here. And with the fame of the three girls, they swarmed here like bees to honey. And the ones I favored most of all were the clergy because they were silent, rich, family men, and understanding. Among them, the Father of Saint Lazarus came here to beg alms. And when he saw this girl, she went to his heart, and in his saintliness and simplicity he asked me to give her to him as his wife.

"So I did, under the following conditions and articles:

"First, he would have to maintain our household, and what we could earn ourselves would go for our clothes and our savings.

"Second, because he was a little decrepit, if my daughter should at any time take on an ecclesiastical assistant, he would be as quiet as if he were at mass.

"Third, that all the children she would have, he would have to take as his own and promise them what he did or might possess.

And if my daughter didn't have any children, he would make her his sole and lawful heir.

"Fourth, that he would not come into our house when he saw a jug, a pot, or any other vessel in the window because that was a signal that there wasn't any place for him.

"Fifth, that when he was in the house and someone else came, he would have to hide where we told him until the other person left.

"Sixth and last, that twice a week he would have to bring us some friend or acquaintance who would provide us with a great feast.

"These are the articles of the marriage contract," she continued, "that that poor wretch and my daughter swore to. The marriage took place without their having to go to a priest because he said it wasn't necessary. The most important part, he said, was for there to be mutual agreement about their wishes and intentions."

I was astonished at what that second Celestina* was telling me and at the marriage contract she had used to marry her daughter. I was confused: I didn't know what to say. But they lit up the road to my desire because the young widow grabbed me around the neck and said, "If that poor fellow had had the face of this angel, I would really have loved him."

And with that she kissed me. After that kiss something started up in me--I don't know what it was--and I began to burn inside. I told her that if she wanted to stop being a widow and take me as her own, I would keep not only the contract of the old man but any other articles she wanted to add. They were happy with that and said they only wanted me to give them everything in the hermitage for safekeeping. I promised to do that, but I intended to hold back the money in case I ever needed it.

The marriage ceremony was to take place the next morning, and that afternoon they sent a cart to take away everything but the nails that held the place together. They didn't overlook the altarcloth or the saint's clothing. I was so bedazzled that if they had asked me for the phoenix or the waters from the river Styx, I would have given it to them. The only thing they left me was a poor piece of sackcloth to lie on like a dog. When that lady--my future wife--who had come with the cart saw that there wasn't any money she was angry. Because the old man had told her that he had some, but he didn't say where. She asked me if I knew where the treasure was. I told her I didn't. Being astute, she took me by the hand so we could go looking for it. She led me to every corner and crevice in the hermitage, including the base of the altar. And when she saw that it had recently been fixed, she became very suspicious.

She hugged and kissed me and said, "My life, tell me where that money is so we can have a happy wedding with it."

I still denied that I knew anything about any money. She took my hand again and led me outside to walk around the hermitage, watching my face all the time. When we got to the place where I had hidden it, my eyes darted there. She called her mother and told her to look under a stone I had put on top of it. She found it, and I found my death.

She feigned a smile and said, "Look. With this we'll have a wonderful life."

She caressed me over and over again, and then, since it was getting late, they went back to the city, telling me to come to their house in the morning and we would have the happiest wedding there had ever been. I hope to God it's full of roses and not thorns, I said to myself.

All that night I was caught between the hope that those women wouldn't trick me and the fear that they would, although I thought it was impossible for there to be any trickery in a woman who had such a good face. I was expecting to enjoy that little pigeon, so the night seemed like a year to me.

It wasn't yet dawn when I closed up my hermitage and went to get married (as if that were nothing), not remembering that I already was. I arrived just as they were getting up. They welcomed me so joyfully that I really thought I was fortunate, and with all my fears gone, I began to act right at home. We ate so well and the food was so good that I thought I was in paradise. They had invited six or seven lady friends of theirs in to eat. After dinner we danced, and although I didn't know how, they made me do it. To see me dancing with my hermit's garb on was a sight.

When evening came, after a good supper and even better drinking, they took me into a nicely decorated room where there was a good bed. They told me to get into it. While my wife was undressing, a maid pulled off my shoes and stockings and told me to take off my shirt because, for the ceremonies that would take place, I had to be completely naked. I obeyed her. Then all the women came into my room with my wife behind them, dressed in a shift, and one of the women was carrying the train.

The first thing they made me do was kiss her arse, saying that was the first ceremony. After this, four of them grabbed me--two by the feet and two by the arms--and with great care they tied four ropes to me and fastened the ends to the four bedposts. I was like a Saint Andrew on the Cross. They all began to laugh when they saw my jack-in-the-box, and they threw a jar of cold water on it. I gave out a terrible shriek, but they told me to be quiet, or else. They took a huge pot of hot water and stuck my head in it. I was burning up, and the worst part was that if I tried to shout they whipped me. So I decided to let them do what they wanted. They sheared off my beard, my hair, my eyebrows and eyelashes.

"Be patient," they said. "The ceremonies will be over soon, and you will enjoy what you desire so much."

I begged them to let me go because my appetite had gone away.

They cut away the hair from my crotch, and one of them who was the boldest took out a knife and said to the others, "Hold him down tight, and I'll cut off his plums so he'll never again feel tempted to get married. This hermit thought everything we told him was the gospel truth. Why, it wasn't even the epistle. He trusted women, and now he'll see what the payment is."

When I saw my precious stones in danger, I pulled so hard that I broke a rope and one of the bedposts. I grabbed my jewels with one hand and clutched them so that even if they had cut off my fingers, they couldn't have gotten to them. So they wouldn't break the bed completely apart, they untied me and wrapped me in a sheet. Then they gave me such a blanketing that they left me half dead.

"These, my dear sir," they said, "are the ceremonies our wedding begins with. If you want to come back tomorrow, we'll finish the rest."

The four of them picked me up and carried me far away from their house. They put me down in the middle of a street. And when morning came, boys began to chase and beat me, so that, to get away from their hands, I ran into a church next to the high altar where they were saying mass. When the priests saw that figure, which must have looked like the devil they paint

at Saint Michael's feet, they began to run away, and I was right behind them, trying to get away from the boys.

The people in the church were shouting. Some said, "Look! There goes the devil!" Others said, "Look at the madman!"

I was shouting, too, but that I wasn't a devil or a madman; I was only a poor fellow who looked like that because of my sins. At this, they all quieted down. The priests went back to their mass, and the sacristan gave me a cover from a tomb to wrap myself in. I went over to a corner and thought about the reverses of fortune and that no matter where you go bad luck is there. So I decided to stay in that church for the rest of my life. And if past misfortunes were any indication, my life wouldn't be a long one. Besides, I wanted to save the priests the trouble of going somewhere else to get me when I was dead.

This, dear reader, is all of the Second Part of the life of Lazarillo. I have neither added nor subtracted anything from what I heard my great-grandmother tell. If you enjoyed it, wait for the Third Part: you will find it no less enjoyable.

*[The unforgettable and infamous old bawd of the Spanish masterpiece *La Celestina* (ca. 1492)--R.S.R.]

Bibliography

Ayala, Francisco. "El 'Lazarillo': Nuevo examen de algunos aspectos." *Cuadernos Américos* 150 (1967): 209-35.

Bataillon, Marcel. *El sentido del Lazarillo de Tormes.* Paris- Toulouse: Librarie des Editions Espagnoles, 1954,

---. *Novedad y fecundidad del Lazarillo de Tormes.* Translated by Luis Cortés Vázquez. Madrid: Ediciones Anaya, 1968.

Boehmer, Eduard. "Juan de Luna." *Zeitschrift fur vergleichende Literaturgeschichte* 15, no. 6 (1904): 423-30.

Caso González, José. *La vida de Lazarillo de Tormes. Boletín de la Real Academia Española.* Anejo 17. (Critical edition, with a preface and notes.) Madrid, 1967.

Castillo, Homero. "El comportamiento de Lázaro de Tormes." *Hispania* 33, no. 4 (1950): 304-10.

Castro, Américo. *El pensamiento de Cervantes. Revista de filología española.* Anejo 6. Madrid, 1925.

---. Hacia Cervantes. Madrid: Taurus Ediciones, 1957.

Chandler, Frank Wadleigh. *The Literature of Roguery*. 2 vols. Boston and New York: Houghton, Mifflin and Co., 1907.

---. *Romances of Roguery*. New York: Burt Franklin, 1961.

Chaytor, H. J. *La vida de Lazarillo de Tormes*. (Introduction and notes in English.) Manchester, England: University Press, 1922.

Cossío, José María de. "Las continuaciones del Lazarillo de Tormes." *Revista de filología española* 25, no. 3 (1941): 514 - 23.

De Haan, Fonger. *An Outline of the History of the Novela Picaresca in Spain*. The Hague and New York: Martinus Nijhoff, 1903.

Díaz-Plaja, Guillermo. *Lazarillo de Tormes: Vida del Buscón don Pablos*. (Preliminary study.) Mexico: Editorial Porrua, 1965.

Gilman, Stephen. "The Death of Lazarillo." *PMLA* 81, no. 3 (1966): 149-66.

González Palencia, Ángel. *Del "Lazarillo" a Quevedo*. Madrid, 1946.

Guillén, Claudio. "La disposición temporal del *Lazarillo de Tormes*." *Hispanic Review* 25, no. 4 (1957): 264-79.

---. *Lazarillo de Tormes and El Abencerraje*. (Introduction and notes in English.) New York: Dell Publishing Co.,1966.

Hesse, Everett W., and Williams, Harry F. *La vida de Lazarillo de Tormes*. (Introduction in English by Américo Castro.) Madison, Wisconsin: University of Wisconsin Press, 1961.

Jones, R. O. *La vida de Lazarillo de Tormes.* (Introduction and notes in English.) Manchester, England: University Press, 1963.

Laurenti, Joseph L. *Estudio crítico de la Segunda Parte de la Vida de Lazarillo de Tormes de Juan de Luna.* Mexico: Ediciones de Andrea, 1965.

Lázaro Carreter, Fernando. "Construcción y sentido del *Lazarillo de Tormes.*" *Ábaco: Estudios sobre literatura española* I (1969): 45-134.

Luna, Juan de. *La Segunda Parte de la Vida de Lazarillo de Tormes.* (Introduction and notes in English by Elmer Richard Sims.) Austin, Texas: University of Texas, 1928.

Piper, Anson C. "The 'Breadly Paradise' of Lazarillo de Tormes." *Hispania* 44, no. 2 (1961): 269-71.

Rico, Francisco. "Problemas del 'Lazarillo.'" *Boletín de la Real Academia Española* 46 (1966): 277-96.

Rudder, Robert S. "La segunda parte de 'Lazarillo de Tormes': La originalidad de Juan de Luna." *Estudios filológicos* 6 (1970): 87-112.

--- "Lazarillo de Tormes y los peces: La continuación anónima de 1555." *Explicación de textos literarios*, 1974.

--- "Lazarillo de Manzanares: A Reconsideration." *Kentucky Romance Quarterly*, 1976.

--- "Nueva luz sobre Juan de Luna." *La picaresca*, ed. Manuel Criado de Val, Madrid, 1979.

Tarr, F. Courtney. "Literary and Artistic Unity in the *Lazarillo de Tormes.*" *PMLA* 42, no. 2 (1927): 404-21.

Wardropper, Bruce. "El trastorno de la moral en el *Lazarillo.*" *Nueva Revista de Filología Hispánica* 15 (1961): 441-47.

Willis, Raymond S. "Lazarillo and the Pardoner: The Artistic Necessity of the Fifth Tractado." *Hispanic Review* 27, no. 3 (1959): 267 – 79.

Other books by Robert S. Rudder

Magic Realism in Cervantes (Translation of work by Arturo Serrano Plaja): Univ. of California Pr.

The Life of Lazarillo de Tormes (Edition and translation): Frederick Ungar Publishing Co.

The Orgy (Edition and translation of Latin American drama): Univ. of California Pr.

The Literature of Spain in English Translation: a Bibliography: Frederick Ungar Publishing Co.

City of Kings (Translation of work by Rosario Castellanos): Latin American Literary Review Pr.

Nazarin (Translation of work by Benito Pérez Galdós): Latin American Literary Review Pr.

The Medicine Man (Translation of work by Francisco Rojas González): Latin American Literary Review Pr.

Solitaire of Love (Translation of work by Cristina Peri Rossi): Duke University Pr.

The Forbidden (Translation of work by Benito Pérez Galdós): Cambridge Scholars Pub.

The Paradox of Saint Teresa of Ávila: A Study in Will and Humility: Edwin Mellen Pr.

Tales of the White Knight: Tirant lo Blanc (Edition and translation of work by Joanot Martorell). Svenson Publishers.

Afternoon of the Dinosaur (Translation of work by Cristina Peri Rossi). Svenson Publishers.

A Dozen Orgies: Latin American Plays of the Twentieth Century (Anthology of one-act dramas in English translation). Svenson Publishers.

Intimate Disasters (Translation of work by Cristina Peri Rossi): Latin American Literary Review Pr. (Forthcoming).

Ebooks by Robert S. Rudder

The Life of Lazarillo de Tormes (Edition and translation).

Tales of the White Knight: Tirant lo Blanc (Edition and translation of work by Joanot Martorell).

La Celestina (Edition in Spanish, with glossary and notes).

Afternoon of the Dinosaur (Translation of work by Cristina Peri Rossi).

The Celestina (Annotated English translation of work by Fernando de Rojas).

A Dozen Orgies: Latin American Plays of the Twentieth Century (Anthology of one-act dramas in English translation).